The Painted War

THE
LAST APPRENTICE

The Painted War

IMOGEN ROSSI

HOT
KEY
BOOKS

With special thanks to Rosie Best

First published in Great Britain in 2014 by Hot Key Books
Northburgh House, 10 Northburgh Street, London EC1V 0AT

Reprinted 2015

A CIP catalogue record for this book is available from the British Library.

ISBN: 978-1-4714-0261-6

This book is typeset in 11pt Sabon using Atomik ePublisher

Printed and bound by Nørhaven, Denmark

Hot Key Books is part of the Bonnier Publishing Group
www.bonnierpublishing.com

For Fiona McLaughlin

Chapter One

Colours swirled in the air like ink dropped into clear water. Thin trails of pigment leaked from the surface of every painting in the throne room of La Luminosa. A beat seemed to pulse behind each one, as if some enormous heart was pumping out the colours. The courtiers who'd been waiting for an audience with Duchess Catriona stared in amazement, muttering and clutching their fans. Even the palace guards' faces were full of wonder.

But Bianca di Lombardi felt nothing but dread.

Somewhere behind those paintings there was another world – Oscurita, the Dark City, where there was no sunlight. And from where the Duchess Edita was about to invade.

Bianca forced herself to turn away from the hypnotic, swirling colours and face her own Duchess. 'They're coming through, right now!' *Please believe me*, she added, to herself.

Duchess Catriona rose from the throne and turned to the Captain of the Guard.

'Captain Raphaeli, call your forces together,' she announced in a clear, fearless voice. 'We must prepare for war.'

Bianca could have wept with relief at the Duchess's trust in her. Without it . . . well, they would be completely unprepared for the battle. The death toll wouldn't bear thinking about.

'Guards! To me!' Captain Raphaeli yelled, jamming a golden helmet down over his thick, curly hair.

Bianca needed to ready herself, too. She looked around the throne room of La Luminosa for something she could use as a weapon. Spotting a long candlestick on a table beside the throne, she picked it up, gripping it like a club. Beside her, Cosimo clenched his fists. Bianca was willing to bet that he hadn't thought his first action as Master Artist of La Luminosa would be to fight an invasion.

'Send word to the barracks,' Captain Raphaeli said. 'Raise the army. Tell them we're under attack from inside the palace.' The armour of the palace guards flashed in the sunlight as they pushed through the crowd of nobles and hurried up the marble steps to the throne. They surrounded the Duchess, Bianca and Cosimo. On Raphaeli's command they drew their swords and held their spears pointing outwards.

Most of the nobles were unarmed. It had been decades since the people of La Luminosa carried weaponry. A few had ornamental daggers, which they drew from their colourful gowns and robes, but they were more for show than for fighting. The nobles gasped and tripped over each other in their attempts to huddle together at the foot of the steps to the throne, standing as close to Raphaeli and the guards as they dared.

'Secretary Franco, come here,' ordered the Duchess. The

guards parted to let an elderly man in a sunflower-yellow robe come to the Duchess's side. He had skin as brown as Bianca's friend Marco's, creased and crinkled in worry lines across his forehead. 'Secretary Franco, how do we defend the city from an attack from the inside?'

'The first thing we need to do', said Secretary Franco, 'is remove Your Highness to the White Tower. And Lady Bianca, too,' he said, with a slightly suspicious glance at Bianca. 'Until her Oscuritan heritage is . . . confirmed.'

Was he calling her a liar? Bianca had only just found out she was the daughter of the *true* Duchess of Oscurita – Saralinda. She might have been raised as an artist's apprentice, but this discovery meant that she was royal through and through.

'Absolutely not,' said Duchess Catriona. 'I will fight for my city and my crown alongside my loyal guards. I'll defend them until my last breath.'

Bianca hefted the candlestick and nodded her agreement. She might be a Lady in Oscurita but she was determined to protect her home and her friends in La Luminosa, no matter what. Even if that meant going to war against her own aunt . . .

'Do not be foolish, Your Highness,' Secretary Franco said. 'You have no heir! Your crown will be worth nothing to any of us if you are killed in the first skirmish. This is not a child's game. This is war!'

Duchess Catriona bristled, and Bianca took an involuntary half-step back.

'You're quite right, Franco,' she snapped. 'I'm no longer a

3

little girl playing heroes at my father's feet. I am your Duchess, and I will face this invasion with my sword in my hand.'

A few of the nobles gasped and fanned themselves, and Bianca scowled at them. They were acting as if they were watching Marco's harlequin troupe performing a play! Franco looked as if he was going to speak again, but Catriona seized her skirts and wheeled around in a flutter of red silk.

'Captain Raphaeli, send for my armour, at once!' she snapped. 'And don't you dare try to convince me to run, too, Raphaeli, I won't hear it!'

'There isn't time,' Captain Raphaeli said. 'Ready your arms, guards,' he commanded. 'We fight for La Luminosa, and for our Duchess!'

A cry went up from the guards, and they raised their spears and swords so that the sharp edges glinted in the sunlight. Suddenly, with a sucking noise, the streams of colour in the air started to retreat. They flowed back into their paintings and vanished.

This is it. Bianca held her breath and clutched the candlestick in her shaking hands. Any second now the magical painted doors would burst open with soldiers in dark plate armour climbing out of the paintings, clutching their pointed silver spears and carrying the deep purple banners of Oscurita . . .

Bianca was ready. She would fight.

But then . . . nothing.

'What . . . What happened?' Cosimo muttered.

'It seems that *nothing* has happened,' said Secretary Franco coolly.

A confused silence descended on the throne room. Bianca's heart pounded in her chest. This had to be a trick. Edita must have a plan, to catch them unawares.

Captain Raphaeli turned to the woman at his side and muttered under his breath, 'Sergeant Forza, I want to know if anything's come through the paintings elsewhere in the city.'

Forza gave him a sharp salute and broke ranks. The sound of her armour clanking as she ran echoed around the hushed throne room.

Then muttering and sighs of relief started to go up from the courtiers huddled at the foot of the steps, and some of the guards lowered their swords.

'Orders, sir?' said one of the soldiers.

Captain Raphaeli didn't lower his sword, but he didn't answer the soldier either.

'Perhaps it was some amusing demonstration,' said Lady Giuliana, snapping open her fan. 'Master Cosimo, have you added even more enchantments to the Duchess's paintings?' Bianca felt her face flush as several of the other nobles looked up at her and Cosimo.

'Artists are eccentrics, after all,' said her companion, putting away a dagger so encrusted with jewels it probably wouldn't even cut through butter. Bianca recognised him: Lord Cassio, one of the Duchess's more slimy and annoying courtiers. He turned and gave Secretary Franco a mocking smile. 'The palace has become a place full of pranks and laughter these days. Perhaps dear young Bianca and Her Glorious Highness have invented this magical dark city to have a little bit of fun with us all. We are all enjoying it very much, are we not?' He gave a forced laugh and looked around at the other courtiers, who faked laughter along with him.

Secretary Franco didn't smile, and neither did Bianca. Her heart was still hammering and her palms on the candlestick were damp with sweat. She glanced around at the paintings, still expecting them to burst open and Oscuritan soldiers to burst through, swords raised.

'This isn't a joke!' she snapped. 'I was there. In Oscurita. Edita opened the ways between the paintings. She *said* she was planning to invade!'

'Come, Bianca, really?' said Lady Giuliana, in an infuriatingly calm voice. 'You expect us to believe in an invading army marching through the paintings?'

'Yes! Cosimo, Your Highness, tell them! Art is my life, these paintings are my family's legacy. I would never say such a thing if it wasn't true.'

'Still,' Duchess Catriona said, in a thoughtful voice that made Bianca's heart sink, 'I see no invaders here. Bianca, are you *sure* about what you saw? There can be no doubt about this. I called for the whole army to be raised. I was about to order the palace emptied and the city evacuated. You realise how much trouble that would've caused the people?'

'I know what I saw and heard,' Bianca said firmly. 'We should still begin evacuating –'

She was cut off by a loud creak and a bang as the doors of the throne room were suddenly thrown open. Captain Raphaeli raised his sword and jumped in front of Catriona.

Bianca turned with her heart in her mouth . . . but it was just a servant, standing in the doorway with a heavy, lumpy bundle in his arms, sweat dripping from his hair and his shoulders shaking as he gasped for breath.

'I bring Your Highness's armour!' he gulped.

Titters of laughter rippled through the crowd of courtiers. Bianca cringed. Catriona's face flushed deep red and then drained of all colour again, her birthmark standing out bright against her cheek. She turned a look of pale, embarrassed fury on the courtiers, and they stopped laughing at once.

The servant carried the carefully wrapped armour up to the throne steps and laid it at Catriona's feet.

'Your Highness,' said Bianca gently. 'We're friends, aren't we? You know I wouldn't lie about this.'

'Your Highness,' Cosimo spoke up – bravely, Bianca thought, considering the look that Duchess Catriona gave him. 'From everything I've seen in the last few hours and everything Marco the tumbler told the apprentices about Oscurita . . . I believe Bianca.'

Bianca heard Lady Giuliana's strident voice again, speaking in a whisper that could be heard all around the room. 'Don't they make a striking pair of advisors for such a young Duchess? An apprentice who claims to be a princess and a master artist barely out of boyhood. Like a group of children playing kings and queens.'

Duchess Catriona stamped her foot. 'Shut up, Giuliana!' She bent down, grabbed a golden gauntlet from the top of the pile of armour and threw it hard across the room. It missed Giuliana and flew into a painting of Queen Verity

7

of Caledonia. The gauntlet hit the Queen squarely in the shoulder and caught the canvas, tearing it right down the middle as it clattered to the ground.

Bianca gasped and her hands flew to her mouth. That painting was one of Master di Lombardi's first great masterpieces.

'Oh . . . Bianca, look what you made me do now,' Catriona said quietly, and shook her head.

Beside her, Secretary Franco let out a long, exasperated sigh. 'Your Highness, you know I have the greatest respect for you. But perhaps if you don't wish your people to think of you as a child, you should try to rise above temper tantrums!' His voice rose, almost to a snarl, and Bianca braced herself for Catriona to use her whole suit of armour as a weapon and hit him with it. But to Bianca's surprise, Duchess Catriona looked at the floor.

'And Lady Bianca, Master Cosimo,' Franco said, turning to them. 'I respect your profession. I know that Lady Bianca has been of great help to the Duchess in the past.' His voice softened, but he was firm. 'But perhaps in the future it would be better if the defence of the city was left up to the Duchess's expert advisors.'

Bianca put her candlestick back down on the table by the throne with a heavy and deliberate *thunk*. 'Duchess Edita still has my mother captive, Secretary Franco. She's mustering the Resistance in Oscurita. I did what I thought was right, and I'm not going to stop doing that just because I've had fewer birthdays than you.' She turned to Duchess Catriona. 'Please be careful, Your Highness. I don't think –'

'Thank you, Bianca, you may go,' said Duchess Catriona.

Bianca's mouth dropped open. She had thought her friend trusted her, but Catriona didn't meet her eyes – she turned to Franco and Raphaeli. 'I want to be absolutely sure that we are safe,' she said. 'If this had been a real invasion, we might have been caught unawares.'

Bianca turned, not waiting for Cosimo, and walked out of the throne room. She had been humiliated. And worse, no one believed exactly how much danger they were in.

Chapter Two

Hurrying footsteps echoed behind Bianca as she stormed along the corridor. She expected Cosimo to be following her from the throne room but a brief, involuntary smile lit her face when she turned and saw Marco instead.

'What's happening?' he asked, drawing level with her. 'Did Edita invade? Is the Duchess all right?'

Bianca sighed. 'There was no invasion – not yet. Half the court thinks Cosimo made the paintings do that as a joke. And the Duchess . . .' She shook her head. 'We're in terrible danger, and I don't know how to make them see it!'

'Take them through to Oscurita,' Marco suggested. 'Show them the passages – one by one, if you have to!'

'We can't risk it,' Bianca muttered. 'All we can do is keep looking for ways to use Master di Lombardi's inventions to fight Edita. Then when she does invade, we'll be able to help.'

Marco whistled under his breath. 'Well, we've found some stuff –'

'Lady Bianca, wait a moment,' called a voice. Bianca turned, and saw Captain Raphaeli hurrying down the corridor towards them. 'A word, please.'

Bianca steeled herself for another ticking off. 'Just . . . Just call me Bianca,' she said. 'I'm not royalty here.'

'Yes, My Lady,' said Raphaeli.

'I was only trying to protect Duchess Catriona, you know,' she said. 'I really thought –'

'I know,' interrupted Raphaeli. 'I believe you.'

Bianca blinked at him. 'You do?'

The top part of Raphaeli's face was obscured by his gleaming golden helmet, but his eyes met hers and she could see the earnest, worried expression in them. 'Can we talk?' the Captain asked again. He glanced at Marco.

'Marco knows everything,' Bianca said.

Raphaeli gave her a short bow and opened a door to his left. It was an empty secretary's office, lined with shelves piled high with scrolls and books bound in leather and brass. Bianca and Marco went inside and Raphaeli closed the door before sighing and lifting off the golden helmet. He shook out his hair and placed the helmet down on top of a pile of books.

'I believe your story . . .' Bianca wasn't expecting that. 'Because I've met someone from Oscurita before.'

Bianca *really* wasn't expecting that. 'Why do you know about it and the other courtiers don't?'

'Because it was kept secret,' said Raphaeli. 'The courtiers who did know about it were jailed by the Baron da Russo when the Duchess's father died. But I was just a young legionary in the palace guard then. I don't think he knew I knew. I wasn't supposed to.'

'When did this happen?' Marco asked.

'It was when the old Duke was coming out of mourning for Catriona's mother.' Raphaeli's hand strayed from the sword at his belt to his throat, twisting a silver chain that was tucked into the neck of his tunic. He didn't seem to know he was doing it. 'I was in the Duke's guard when the painting opened,' he said. 'It was nothing like what happened today. The door in the picture just swung open and there were people on the other side! It was incredible . . . A whole world, just beyond the paintings.' Bianca smiled a little, remembering her first time in the secret passages.

'A diplomatic party had come from the Dark City, to forge an alliance with La Luminosa,' said Raphaeli. 'Master di Lombardi was leading them, with an apprentice and a few other nobles. They spoke to the Duke, left quietly, and never came back. Most of the Luminosan courtiers never knew who they really were.'

'There are good and bad people in Oscurita, just like La Luminosa,' said Bianca with a half-smile. '*This* visit from Oscurita isn't going to be friendly – Edita's after conquest, not diplomacy. She fooled me once – I'm not going to be fooled again.' She met Raphaeli's eyes and clasped her hands together, ready to plead if she had to. 'You *must* be vigilant, Captain. The whole city depends on it.'

'I will,' said the Captain seriously. 'I promise.' The silver chain sneaked out of his tunic as he turned to leave, and Bianca saw a golden ring on the chain. It was engraved with a twisting ivy pattern, which glinted as he walked away.

'Bianca!' Domenico and Sebastiano looked up as Bianca and Marco opened the door to Master di Lombardi's secret workshop. Bianca sighed, relaxing a little bit just at the sight of the place. You could have fitted a small house inside the room easily, and almost every inch was taken up with workbenches and tools, paints and canvases, half-finished works of art and strange inventions. Brass, copper, glass and leather gleamed in the warm sunlight that flooded down into the room from the enormous skylight windows high above.

She could tell the three boys had been busy – half the drawers and cabinets were open, neat piles of notebooks and sketches were stacked on all the workbenches. Sebastiano was kneeling beside a large contraption with a glass dome and two seats inside – di Lombardi's Vehicle for Travelling Underneath the Canal Surface. Domenico was sitting in the cockpit of the flying machine, tinkering with its controls. Bianca hoped it could be made to work again – a flying machine might be their best advantage over the army of Oscurita.

'I don't care if they think I'm a liar,' Bianca said once Marco had finished telling Domenico and Sebastiano what had happened. 'I know the truth. Edita's going to invade. It's just a matter of when. And she's still got my mother, locked up in that terrible tower.' She scraped her hair back from her face and twisted it at the back of her neck nervously, remembering the dark, freezing Tower of Thorns. Its chill wind cut through the glassless windows and the razor-sharp metal spikes that stuck out could slice anyone who tried to climb to freedom out of the windows. 'If Edita finds out we escaped the tower, my mother will be hidden away so the Resistance can't rescue her. She might even kill her. I've got to go back.'

Marco winced. 'I don't know, Bianca. What if that's Edita's plan? What if she's luring you back into her clutches?'

Bianca shook her head. 'What if she's not?' She turned to Domenico. 'You and Seb keep looking for ways we can use the inventions to fight an invasion.'

Domenico climbed out of the flying machine and patted its wooden and copper surface. 'You can rely on us, Bianca.' Sebastiano nodded.

'All right.' Marco shrugged. 'Let's go.'

'No, stay here,' Bianca said. 'Think about it – you're the only other person in La Luminosa who knows what Edita looks like.' Bianca rolled her shoulders back, steeling herself. 'If my aunt does catch me, Duchess Catriona will need you.'

'Well, that's bleak,' muttered Marco, but he didn't try to contradict her. He squeezed her shoulder. 'Don't suppose I can persuade you not to go?'

Bianca shook her head.

'All right. Find your mum and come straight back, OK?'

'I will,' said Bianca, praying it would be that simple.

Bianca reached into the leather pouch at her belt and took out the paintbrush that Master di Lombardi had left to her. She stared at it for a moment. Since her Master had first pressed it into her hand she had discovered the secret passages, driven a flying machine, destroyed a fake duchess and discovered a whole other world where it was always night and she was a princess – and found out her master was really her own grandfather. All that, with the power of a very special paintbrush.

close to her lips and whispered, 'Hidden rooms,

14

secret passages, second city.' The brush gave its familiar whirring and clicking, and the side of the handle slid away to let the small copper key fold out into place. She slid it into the lock and let herself out of di Lombardi's studio.

It didn't take Bianca very long to find the place in the secret passages where she had painted her way out of the Tower of Thorns – she'd recognise the only door she'd created anywhere.

She reached out and gripped the handle. The sensation was odd under her fingers – the handle felt strangely crumbly, like the stone wall it'd been painted onto, not the smooth, stiff texture of painted canvas that made up the rest of the secret passages.

With a gasped breath, she pulled it open and leaned through into the dark, cold tower cell on the other side.

For a moment, even with Bianca's sharp, half-Oscuritan eyesight, the room was so dark that she couldn't see if her mother was inside. But then there was a gasp and a light flared – a blue bolt of lightning, trapped in an orb of glass. Its cold, flickering light lit the face of the rightful Duchess Saralinda, sitting upright and alert on her plain bed. She leapt to her feet with the thunder lamp clutched in her hands, rushing across the sparse cell she had occupied for almost thirteen years.

'Bianca,' said Saralinda, enfolding her in a tight hug. 'You've come back!'

'You've got to come with me,' Bianca said, her voice muffled in the sleeve of her mother's plain black gown. 'Edita didn't invade through the paintings. I don't know what her plan is but you are in danger here!' She pulled away and met Saralinda's eyes. Her mother's face had gone soft and sad – she looked as if she was about to say she couldn't come back to La Luminosa. Bianca was ready for this. 'You can stay in the secret passages between the paintings so that you won't be harmed by the Luminosian sunlight. Di Lombardi – I mean, Grandfather – he painted Duchess Catriona a special room to hide in, inside his workshop. You can stay there!'

Saralinda smiled, but it was a rueful smile, and she squeezed Bianca's hand as she did so.

Bianca's heart sank. 'You won't come?'

'I couldn't leave with you and my father thirteen years ago, and I'm not leaving now. I stayed to fight Edita's cruel reign. This is my city, Bianca, and it's still being ruled by a tyrant.'

Bianca felt a strange smile creep over her face. She wasn't happy, but she did feel proud. 'You sound like Duchess Catriona,' she said. *Except less shouty.*

'A duchess's duty is to fight for her people, no matter what.'

'But can you really fight for them from this room?' Bianca pleaded. 'You need to get out of here right now! If Edita . . .' She trailed off, trying desperately not to imagine Edita's temper breaking, her guards seizing Saralinda and dragging her to the window, the razor-sharp thorns, the long drop . . .

'You're right,' said Saralinda, and Bianca blinked up at her. 'Am I?'

'I've been working with the Resistance, waiting for them to decide when the time is right to break me out and strike

16

for the throne.' Bianca's mother had a strange twinkle in her eye. 'I think that time is now. The time is right for me to rejoin my loyal subjects.'

Bianca pulled out the paintbrush key with a smile. Saralinda planted a brief, heartfelt kiss on Bianca's forehead and took the key from her hand.

'Follow me,' Bianca's mother said, seizing a black woollen shawl and wrapping it around her shoulders. 'We must be as quick and as quiet as shadows.'

Bianca felt a flush of warmth spreading over her from the place her mother had kissed her.

They started down the endless, spiralling stairs within the Tower of Thorns, and Bianca tried to breathe and tread as softly as she could. The only other sound was the whistling of the wind through the tiny slit windows and in the quiet her feet seemed to slap on the stone and her breath rasped in her throat. The stairs went on and on, around and around, until Bianca had no idea how far they'd gone. Saralinda was running her hand over the wall as they went. Bianca had assumed it was for balance, but suddenly her mother stopped and turned to the wall, stroking it with her palm.

'Here,' she murmured. 'It's here.'

Bianca stared at the wall. It looked like an ordinary wall, but Bianca had seen enough magic in painting to know never to trust her eyes.

Her mother's fingers found a tiny chink between the giant stone bricks in the wall, and she slipped the key in. It turned with a little *click* and part of the wall slid back with a sound like grinding, crumbling stone.

What surprised Bianca was that the hidden passage wasn't painted, or apparently magical at all – it was a real door built into the building. The dark space on the other side was a thin, gently sloping corridor made from the same dark stone as the rest of the castle.

'Where does it go?' Bianca asked her mother.

'Behind the barracks, into the castle itself.' Bianca let out a long breath. Saralinda put a steadying hand on her shoulder. 'It'll be OK. I know where I'm going.'

'Are there lots of these passages, then?' Bianca asked to take her mind off the idea of walking right past the barracks where Edita's soldiers slept.

'All over the castle,' said Saralinda. 'I know them all by heart – after all, I was Duchess once. And before that, I was a little girl who loved exploring,' she added, with a fond smile. She led the way into the corridor and slid the heavy stone door back into place behind them.

The darkness was almost total, and Bianca was very glad to feel Saralinda's hand slip into hers as they started down the incline.

'Things were different back then,' Saralinda whispered. 'It must be hard to imagine, but this place was so beautiful, full of laughter and music and art. The fireplaces burned a different colour in every room, and the choirs never stopped singing . . .' She stopped walking and turned back to Bianca. She could just make out the shape of her pale face and the grey streaks in her dark hair as she put her finger to her lips. Bianca nodded, and looked past Saralinda to see a flight of dark steps striped with thin beams of light.

As Saralinda led her carefully and silently down the steps, Bianca paused to put her eye to a tiny hole in the wall. She could see down into a firelit chamber lined with neat, low beds and racks on the walls that looked like they might hold spears, swords and axes. The room was deserted.

Around the corner Bianca heard a rhythmical, metallic clanking echoing from the other side of the wall. She put her eye to another small hole in the stone wall and stifled a gasp.

She'd found the soldiers! Bianca and her mother were in the walls surrounding the enormous courtyard, looking down into it from above. The courtyard was lit with more crackling thunder lamps. Their dancing, flickering blue-and-white light glinted off the polished silver armour and wickedly sharp-looking spears of hundreds and hundreds of soldiers. They were lined up in neat rows, standing elbow to elbow and running drills in perfect unison. Her chest seemed to tighten, squeezing her heart painfully. She was sure that La Luminosa didn't have as many soldiers as this – certainly not trained, armed and ready for battle. She prayed that Captain Raphaeli was doing something about that right now . . .

Saralinda gently put a hand on Bianca's shoulder and led her to the end of the corridor, where there was a wooden door. 'We have to be brave, now,' she whispered. 'We're heading for the battlements. But first, we need to pass by the door to the throne room.'

Bianca pulled away and stared at her mother, eyes widening.

'There's no other way,' whispered Saralinda. 'We just have to walk past the doors with confidence, and draw no attention to ourselves.'

Bianca felt as if she'd swallowed a stick of di Lombardi's chalk and it'd stuck in her throat, drying it and making it impossible to breathe properly.

Saralinda slipped the key into the lock. The wooden door creaked as she opened it, painfully loud. Saralinda stepped out and Bianca screwed up her courage and followed.

They came out in an alcove that opened onto the wide hall right outside the throne room. Bianca shrank back as she saw that the hall was busy – servants, guards and Edita's courtiers crossed the black-and-white tiled floor, most walking quickly with their heads down.

Are they hurrying to prepare for the invasion?

Saralinda took off her black woollen shawl and handed it to Bianca, who folded it and draped it over her head, hoping it'd hide the fact that she and her mother looked so alike.

'Won't they recognise you?' she whispered.

'I've been locked away for so long,' Saralinda said. All the same, she ran her hands through her long hair so that it swung forward over her eyes. Then she took a deep breath and walked out of the alcove with a quick step, keeping her eyes to the ground. Bianca tried to copy her, imagining she was a servant with an important task to be done somewhere else in the castle.

Brighter light spilled out through the huge doors to the throne room, and Bianca heard voices that made her stomach clench and her hands shake: Duchess Edita, talking with the traitors Piero Filpepi and Baron da Russo.

I am a servant, I am allowed to be here, I'm just going about my business . . . Bianca repeated the thoughts over and over, tugging the shawl a little lower over her forehead, hoping to hide her face. And then she stepped into the light. Bianca couldn't help herself: she looked into the throne room. Edita was surrounded by more guards in glinting silver armour, listening with narrowed eyes as the Baron da Russo spoke to her. She was turning something over and over in her hands that glinted as it spun.

My medallion! The one di Lombardi had left to Bianca in his will, the one Edita had stolen from her and used to open the passages between the two cities. Bianca gritted her teeth and her pace slowed to a shuffle. If only she could listen and find out exactly what Edita was planning . . .

A frantic movement distracted Bianca and she looked up to see Saralinda at the foot of the steps, beckoning her to move, her face drawn and fearful. Bianca took a few quick half-running steps forward and Saralinda held up her hand with a wince. Just as Bianca remembered to walk smoothly, Edita's voice rang out.

'Who was that? Shut up, da Russo. Who's that child? Guards, fetch her to me at once!'

Bianca swallowed a curse and broke into a run. Saralinda hitched up her skirt and started up the stairs, hesitating every few steps until Bianca had drawn level with her. 'Up, then left, to the long gallery,' she said as Bianca passed her.

There was a clanking of armour behind them. 'Halt!'

'Don't look back!' Saralinda said. Bianca fixed her eyes on the landing at the top of the stairs and sprinted for it, leaping up the stairs as if they were made of hot iron. The clanking got louder. She grabbed the stone balustrade at the top and pulled herself up onto the landing, looking back for just a second to see six armoured guards rushing towards the stairs, spear-points first.

Saralinda grabbed Bianca's hand and dragged her away. Turning left, they ran along the landing, passing the open doors of rooms and shoving aside courtiers who turned to stare at them as they hurtled by. Bianca's shawl flapped behind her like the wings of a great black bird.

A bewildered servant stood between them and the door to the long gallery, a pitcher of water in her hands. Saralinda snatched the pitcher as they passed and threw it to the floor. It smashed, splashing water across the smooth stone floor. Bianca didn't look back, but as they reached the end of the long corridor she heard the clanking armour hit the ground with a crash and a volley of Oscuritan curses. Saralinda tore open the door to the long gallery, and Bianca grinned up at her mother as they ran through.

She ran right into something hard, and staggered back. Saralinda gasped and put her arms around Bianca's shoulders to stop her from falling. Bianca looked up: from the shiny silver breastplate engraved with trailing ivy, to the deep blue cloak spilling over the guard's shoulders, to the grimly set mouth and narrowed eyes, and finally to the tip of his viciously pointed spear. The door swung shut behind them with a heavy and very final *thud*.

Chapter Three

Bianca drew herself up, showing the guardsman her best brave face. There was a fairly good chance he wouldn't run her through where she stood. Edita would probably want them alive – for now. She sucked in a deep breath and stepped in front of Saralinda.

'Run,' she told her mother.

Bianca heard the quiet click of a key turning in a lock. She glanced back. Saralinda had locked the door behind them.

She's right, the two of us can take him! Bianca readied herself to grab hold of his spear . . . but the guard's grim face melted into a smile. He pointed his spear towards the ground and gave a low bow.

'Your Highness,' he said. 'I take it we're just in time.'

'Perfect, as always, Lieutenant Pietro,' said Saralinda. She stepped past Bianca, who watched with a slightly glazed smile as her mother gave the guardsman a quick, friendly hug.

'You're too kind, Your Highness,' said Pietro.

Relief flooded through Bianca. 'So, we're OK?'

Saralinda grinned. 'Bianca, this is Lieutenant Pietro – he's with the Resistance. He joined the castle guard as a spy.

Pietro, this is my daughter, Bianca.'

'Nice to meet you,' Bianca said, and felt herself blush a tiny bit as Pietro swept a low bow to her. He smiled as he straightened up and opened his mouth to say something, but he was interrupted by clattering, banging and shouting from behind the door.

'Open this door! In the name of the Duchess!' shouted one of the guards on the other side.

'Quickly,' said Pietro, lowering his voice. 'They'll be coming around the other way.' He turned with a sweep of his blue cloak and beckoned for Bianca and her mother to follow. They hurried about halfway down the long gallery until Pietro stopped and tapped a couple of times on the wall, then nodded to Saralinda. Bianca spotted the slight crack in the plaster just before her mother opened the hidden door with the magical paintbrush key. There were dark, tightly spiralling stairs beyond going both up and down. Pietro led them down. A hot, damp blast of air hit Bianca in the face as she turned a corner. There had to be laundry going on nearby – she'd always helped Mistress Quinta with the washing when there was a lot to do, and she'd never forget the distinctive smell of steam, ash and bubbling starch.

Sure enough, Pietro pushed the door open onto a deserted room lined with six huge tubs full of soaking linen. They'd emerged through another of Oscurita's hidden doors – real, but painted to look just like the wall.

'Hurry, the servants could be back any minute,' said Pietro.

At the end of the room there was a drying rack piled high with neatly folded dark cloth, and Saralinda started searching through the piles. She pulled out an itchy-looking piece of grey wool and tossed it to Bianca, who unfolded it and discovered it was a headdress.

'It'll be a better disguise than that old shawl,' Saralinda said. 'Here, put this on over your dress.' She held out a matching plain grey servant's dress and Bianca dragged it on over her head, grateful that it completely covered her cream La Luminosan clothes. 'Now, hold these.' She held out a heavy pile of folded black sheets and Bianca took them. 'There – now you're a laundry girl.'

Saralinda picked out a dress for herself, just as plain and grey as Bianca's, but she added a thick black leather apron and tucked her long hair inside a close-fitting cook's cap.

'How do we look?' she asked Pietro.

'Wonderfully ordinary, Your Highnesses,' Pietro replied. 'Are you ready?'

Saralinda raised her eyebrows at Bianca and she adjusted her headdress once more, and then nodded. Then Pietro opened the laundry door and led the way out through the servants' quarters.

Just like the rest of the castle, the tight corridors and dim rooms that they passed through were crowded with people bustling about, getting ready for . . . something. Bianca tried to keep her eyes focused on her armful of laundry, but she couldn't help pricking her ears for any hint of Edita's plan.

Pietro strode in front of them and they followed in his wake as the other servants sprang out of his way. One girl was about her age, wearing the same grey servant's uniform and headdress. She gave a slightly annoyed roll of her eyes as

Pietro passed and Bianca realised that the girl's life probably wasn't much different from the life of a servant in the palace of La Luminosa.

Edita may be wicked but if this girl refused to work for her how long would it take her to starve? The thought nagged at Bianca as she bustled past the girl and followed Pietro through the hot, busy kitchens and out into a chilly courtyard full of stamping horses and scurrying stablehands. *Loyal or not, these are our subjects. They're not my enemies.*

'The Baron's steed is ready,' said a voice. 'But I don't understand – are you *sure* we don't need to prepare more than one?'

Bianca almost tripped over a cobblestone as she looked around the stableyard, searching for the source of the voice. She found it – a young woman in a leather jerkin and high boots was standing by a pitch-black steed, which wore a bright ruby-red bridle and a saddle encrusted with jewels.

Bianca frowned, ducking behind a tall mounting-block to hide her face while she listened. She didn't know anything about horses in battle, but she was sure this tack was a lot more flashy than protective. Would the Baron really be riding it into a fight?

She risked peering around the block. The stablehand was talking to a man who was dressed as showily as the horse, in the Oscuritan fashion Bianca had come to know – a nearly-black blue robe that swept the ground behind him, trimmed with very bright blue silk.

'Are you questioning your orders, stable girl?' he sneered.

'No, sir! One horse for the Baron's sortie, sir!' The

stablehand snapped to attention and fired off a salute.

'You, laundry girl!' Pietro suddenly snapped, and Bianca almost dropped her laundry in a pile of horse dung. She looked up and saw Pietro giving her an exaggerated angry look. 'Stop slacking. Mistress Flavia wants those sheets at once!' he barked.

'Yes, sir!' Bianca yelped, and ran after him.

Saralinda was waiting for them at a small door on the other side of the courtyard. 'What were you doing?' she muttered to Bianca.

'That woman said something about a horse for the Baron,' Bianca whispered back. 'I didn't hear enough,' she added with a frown. 'They said they only wanted one horse, but that doesn't make any sense . . . Why would they only want one horse for a whole army?'

CLONG! CLONG! CLONG!

Bianca looked up, her heart in her mouth, as a bell rang out somewhere above her.

'That's the alarm,' said Pietro. 'Go, quickly.' He opened the door and Saralinda slipped out.

Bianca cast a last glance back at the glossy black horse, then heard voices shouting. She caught the words 'pretender', 'escape', and 'find them'.

Bianca quickly turned away and followed Saralinda out of the courtyard, down a dark and steeply sloping cobbled alleyway where black-thorned ivy grew between the bricks of the walls. Light crackled at the end of the alley, and Bianca sucked in a deep breath of cool air as she stepped onto an ordinary street outside the castle.

If anything, the bells sounded even louder outside the castle. As Bianca, Saralinda and Pietro crossed a bridge over the canal, they passed a pair of women carrying black wicker baskets who'd stopped to stare up at the bell tower, muttering to each other. Then they hurried on their way, their pale Oscuritan faces taking on a sickly greenish look.

'Why do they look so afraid?' Bianca whispered to her mother. 'It's not them Edita's looking for.'

'The bells mean trouble for somebody,' said Saralinda grimly. 'And if Edita doesn't find whoever she's hunting, she'll take their friends, or their relatives, or just some poor soul who was in the wrong place at the wrong time.'

Bianca glanced at Pietro, and didn't find any comfort in his face. The muscles in his jaw worked as he gritted his teeth.

'We were hoping to get you out as soon as we heard Edita had opened the passages, but she doubled the guard on the Tower. I'd hoped to have longer to get you to . . .' He walked around a corner in front of her and then backed up so quickly she almost walked into him. He held his spear out to stop Saralinda turning the corner. 'Wait here,' he whispered.

Bianca and Saralinda huddled close to the wall as he adjusted his cloak and walked on, at a sort of hurried strolling pace.

'Ho there, friend,' Bianca heard him call out. 'What's all this racket from the castle? Has a prisoner escaped?'

'Haven't you heard? The pretender's got out of her tower. All units are ordered to drop everything until she's found,' replied a woman's voice.

'God's teeth!' Pietro swore.

Bianca edged carefully to the corner of the building and risked a glance down the street. Pietro was striding towards a soldier who stood below a thunder lamp, her silver armour flickering and reflecting the crackling bolts of light. Bianca pulled back quickly, listening hard to catch Pietro's conversation.

'The daughter might be with her, too,' said the guard.

'That little brat's given us no end of trouble,' said Pietro. 'I'd like to wring her scrawny neck.'

'You might get to,' chuckled the guard. 'New orders from the Duchess – she wants them brought back, and she doesn't much care if they're breathing.'

Bianca shuddered. Saralinda put her arms around Bianca's shoulders, giving her a quick squeeze. Bianca wished she felt more reassured.

'Humph,' Pietro chuckled. 'Let's hope they put up a fight, then! I'd better be off and get my troops together.'

'Want some company? I'm headed back to barracks myself.' Bianca clenched her fists and held her breath, ready to turn and run – but Pietro spoke again.

'Nah. Better split up. We can cover more ground.'

'True. Good luck, then,' said the guard, and Bianca risked another brief glance into the street to see Pietro turn back towards them. Mercifully, the guard turned the other way and her dark cloak swished around a corner and vanished.

Pietro hurried back to them. 'That was close,' he said. 'I'm afraid I have to get back to my rounds or I'll be missed. Can you make it from here, My Lady?'

'I can,' said Saralinda. 'But first, let's get Bianca home.'

'Hey,' Bianca protested, 'I'm not leaving you now!'

'Oh yes you are,' her mother said.

'But I can't leave you here and not even know if you're safe!'

'Dear Bianca,' said Saralinda. She reached up and tucked a strand of Bianca's hair back behind her servant's headdress. The warmth of her hand on Bianca's cold cheek made Bianca shiver. 'If they find you here, they will kill you. I'd rather you were far away from me and safe, than dead by my side. I know you know it's the only sensible course,' she added, with a look that cut deep into Bianca's heart.

Her mother was right – Bianca did know this was the only way. But still, she *couldn't* go – she felt as if her shoes were weighed down with heavy rocks.

'I can't,' she said. 'Not without some idea of how to find you again.'

'If you have absolutely no choice,' her mother said, 'go to Dante's Grocery, near the Cathedral – that's just near the square with Father's statue. Do you think you can find it?'

Bianca thought hard – when she'd visited Oscurita in her dreams she'd found her way to the statue of Annunzio di Lombardi, surrounded by glowing *lux aurumque* flowers. She was sure she could make her way back and find this grocer. She nodded.

'Go into Dante's shop and say "God bless the true Duchess" to Dante. Then cross yourself like this.' Saralinda touched her eyes, her heart and both shoulders in turn. Bianca repeated the motion. 'He'll lead you to the Resistance.'

Bianca nodded.

'Promise me you won't come back here until the danger has passed.'

'I promise.'

'Good girl,' said Saralinda, and her eyes suddenly welled with tears. Lieutenant Pietro looked away politely as she gathered Bianca back into another hug. 'Please be safe,' she whispered, pressing the paintbrush key into Bianca's hand. 'I couldn't bear it if –' She broke off as a sound that chilled Bianca to the bone filled the air – a rhythmical, metallic clanking.

Soldiers!

Bianca pulled away quickly; there was no time. She had to leave.

'God bless the true Duchess,' said Pietro, with a wry smile, and turned to walk towards the approaching sound with a sweep of his cloak. Saralinda placed a single kiss on the top of Bianca's head and hurried off in the opposite direction along the canalside. She didn't look back.

Bianca steeled herself, brushed down her servant's costume, and strode out into the pools of lamplight towards the bridge over the canal.

She glanced back across the canal as she got to the other side, and saw the column of gleaming silver soldiers marching down the street, right past where she'd been standing with Saralinda and Pietro. The sharp points of the soldiers' spears glinted, and Bianca felt the blood rush to her cheeks as she imagined those soldiers rushing through the streets of La Luminosa.

She had to get back and tell Duchess Catriona and Captain Raphaeli what she'd seen. But her heart sank as she realised she had no more proof than she had before.

Will they ever believe me?

Chapter Four

Bianca found the Duchess in her chambers. She was in the middle of an art lesson with Lucia and Cosimo. Marco was there, too, standing on one leg practising juggling oranges. He stuffed them in his pockets when Bianca entered. Guards stood to attention around the room, and Bianca was glad there were at least some precautions in place. She rushed over to where Catriona sat in front of an easel, holding a stick of chalk. 'Duchess,' Bianca said. 'I have just come back from Oscurita. I have seen more evidence that Edita is about to invade!'

'Been off playing princess again, Bianca?' said Lucia. 'Is that why you're so late for work? Because it's too beneath you now?'

Bianca couldn't hide her annoyance. 'I do not think it's beneath me! I love my work!'

'Mistress Lucia,' said Duchess Catriona. Her voice was sweet and calm, but Bianca could hear 'remember who's the Duchess here' echoing under every syllable. 'I know Bianca would never give up her studies, any more than I would.'

Lucia shot Bianca a mean look, but didn't say any more.

'As you say, Your Highness.'

'Bianca, I want to hear more. What did you see?'

Bianca told her everything. Her escape with her mother. The raided alarm that caused panic all over Oscurita. The rows and rows of soldiers readying themselves for attack. She finished her story and silence followed: she looked round at all the disbelieving faces in the room – even the guards were casting strange glances down at her. All except Marco, whose face seemed frozen in an expression of horror. He must be feeling guilty for not coming with her to Oscurita.

'I believe you, Bianca.' Catriona was stern. 'But you will be glad to know that Captain Raphaeli has conducted a review of our armed forces. He ordered his lieutenants to ensure that if the city *was* under threat, we would be able to defend ourselves. There is not a lot more I can do.'

Bianca was eased a little. She knew that Captain Raphaeli was on her side.

'In fact,' said Catriona, giving her a consoling look, 'I've been observing training drills all morning.'

'Thank goodness,' Bianca said. She ignored the exaggerated eye-roll that Lucia gave.

The door to the room opened and Secretary Franco came in, followed by Captain Raphaeli. The sight of the tall, golden-helmed Captain of the Guards calmed Bianca's nerves a little. Franco bowed low to Duchess Catriona. 'Your Highness, I have some business I must discuss with you.'

'Can you discuss while I draw?' Catriona said.

'Of course,' said Secretary Franco slowly, in a voice that sounded more like 'oh lord, must we?' to Bianca. He folded his hands behind his back and leaned over slightly. 'Your Highness, I believe I have found someone who will help us with the canals. You remember that the Master of Canals reported last week that they're in dire need of cleaning – one of the nastier legacies of the Baron da Russo's reign.'

'I remember,' said Duchess Catriona. 'You've done as I said and rounded up some lords and ladies to help pay for it?'

'Just one lord, in fact,' said Secretary Franco. 'Lord Aquarion. I think he'll put up enough money so that we can clear all the canals before the year's out.'

'Oh,' Duchess Catriona sighed. 'Did it *have* to be Lord Aquarion? He's always slightly damp and he smells of fish!' Bianca stifled a smile, but she heard a snigger and looked up to see Lucia covering her mouth with one hand.

Ha! Bianca thought. *You're not so perfectly uptight and professional after all.*

'Lord Aquarion takes a direct interest in the running of his merchant ships,' Secretary Franco pointed out. 'He is a very rich, very practical man.'

Duchess Catriona gave Secretary Franco a sharp look. 'And what does Lord Aquarion want in return for this civic generosity?'

'He seems to want to discuss the matter with you directly,' said Secretary Franco. 'Your Highness, I must say, you would do a lot more good for the city if you gave up these art lessons and spent more time with citizens . . . citizens like Lord Aquarion.'

'No!' Bianca said, before she realised what she was doing. The word almost seemed to echo around the Duchess's sitting room and Cosimo, Lucia, Franco, Marco and Catriona all turned to stare at her. 'I . . . I'm very sorry, Your Highness, I didn't mean to shout,' she said. She gave a little curtsey towards Secretary Franco and the Duchess, for good measure. 'It's just that these lessons aren't just frivolous entertainments. I know the canals are really important, but your education is important, too, just as important as pandering to Lord Aquarion. Art is as important as any other subject – what would La Luminosa be without its art? What would we have to fight for?' She turned to Cosimo with a pleading expression.

'I would prefer it if the Duchess's lessons weren't interrupted,' said Cosimo, but he shook his head at Bianca. 'But it isn't your place to say so,' he added with a stern glare. 'I apologise for Bianca's outburst.'

Well, were you going to say anything? Bianca thought. La Luminosa was nothing without art. Was she the only one to see it?

'Perhaps we can discuss it another time,' Secretary Franco said, giving Bianca a look that said 'some time when you're not here to argue' as clearly as if he'd said it aloud. He turned back to Duchess Catriona and started talking about the canals again. Lucia stepped close to Bianca and looked down her nose at her.

'You're not even our most senior apprentice, remember?' she muttered. 'By rights, Ezio should be here, or Rosa. You and the tumbler are only in these lessons because you're Duchess Catriona's . . . friends.' She gave a sneer on the word 'friends' and Bianca flushed, guessing that if they were alone,

Lucia would have said 'lackeys' or 'hangers-on' instead.

Bianca clenched her teeth, trying to stop herself from snapping back at Lucia. 'Of course, Mistress Lu—'

The room was lit with a strange flash. Bianca tensed.

Is this it? Are they here? She readied herself, searching the room for a weapon.

'What on earth was that?' Duchess Catriona demanded, cutting Secretary Franco off in mid-sentence. There was a rattling of armour as the guards around the room looked about. Captain Raphaeli sprang to the Duchess's side, drawing his sword.

It was as if lightning had struck just outside the window – but it was the middle of a clear, sunny Luminosan day.

There was another flash, even brighter. It filled the room with sharp, strange shadows for a moment and Bianca was oddly reminded of the thunder lamps on the streets of Oscurita. Then the light was gone again.

Bianca spun around, checking the magical paintings on the walls, expecting to see soldiers in silver armour burst out and surround them – but it wasn't the paintings that caught her eye this time.

'Duchess, look!'

On the wall right behind the Duchess, a large mirror hung in an ornate golden frame. But it wasn't just polished metal and glass any more – a soft white light was shining from it.

Duchess Catriona looked over her shoulder and leapt to her feet, sending the chalks on her lap scattering across the floor with a clatter and a spray of rainbow-coloured dust.

'What is it?' She looked to Bianca, and Bianca swallowed.

'I . . . I don't know. I haven't seen anything like it,' she admitted.

'Useless,' Lucia muttered, not quite under her breath.

'Stand back, Your Highness,' said Captain Raphaeli, putting himself between Catriona and the mirror. To his credit, Secretary Franco quickly stood beside him.

They all stared as something appeared on the mirror's surface. Silver writing, elaborate and formal, as if it was being written by an invisible hand.

Her Royal Highness, Edita Ellana Lombardi di Oscurita.

A vision appeared in the mirror underneath the words – a vision of Duchess Edita, as if she was standing in front of the mirror and her face was being reflected back at them. She looked regal and beautiful, with her silver tiara glittering on her head and dark hair caught up in dripping silver chains and deep purple jewels. There was a gentle smile on her lips. Bianca shuddered, remembering the sweet, kindly smile Edita had used to convince her that they were mother and daughter.

More writing snaked over the bottom half of the mirror, and Bianca held her breath, not knowing whether she wanted it to stop or to write faster.

After more than a decade of forced separation,
Duchess Edita is eager to make the acquaintance
of Oscurita's historic allies, the rulers of the great
city of La Luminosa. She sends this message in
a spirit of friendship, to announce the arrival
of a trusted friend and diplomat to help broker

a new and lasting bond between our two sister
cities. Her Highness begs Her Highness Duchess
Catriona of La Luminosa to receive her visitor in
the same spirit of friendship.

The message ended and the words and the picture of Edita
stayed on the surface of the mirror, glowing faintly.

Bianca frowned. It had to be some sort of trick, but she
couldn't see what Edita would gain from announcing her
arrival like this. Captain Raphaeli would have time to rally
the troops and Catriona could be taken somewhere safe . . .

Duchess Catriona read the message and then read it again.
Bianca could see her eyes scanning the words, as if she was
searching them for something. Then the Duchess turned to
Secretary Franco. 'How do I respond?' she asked.

'*Respond?*' Bianca gasped. 'You're not thinking of *replying*
to this are you?'

'Bianca, be quiet!' Lucia snapped.

Bianca shook her head. 'Duchess, this is obviously some
kind of trap, you'd be crazy –'

'Lady Bianca!' Secretary Franco raised his voice until it
almost echoed around the large chamber. 'You are not the
Duchess's court advisor, you are a hot-headed child. And
you *will* allow the Duchess to make rational decisions or
by God – princess or not – I will have you removed from
the palace!'

'Rational –' Bianca began, but she swallowed the rest
of her protest. The painted mural on the wall beside the
mirror had started to pulsate, like the ones in the throne

room in Oscurita when the medallion was first used. It was a painting of a balcony looking out over a rolling, animated landscape of fields and vineyards with lazily circling buzzards overhead. As Bianca watched, the green, cream and copper leaked out into the air in thin streams, and then abruptly seemed to be sucked back into the painting, making it even brighter and more colourful than before.

A trumpet sounded, distantly, and the painted door on one side of the balcony opened.

Bianca gasped and took a step back.

With a clatter of hooves, the Baron da Russo rode through the doorway on the back of the enormous black stallion – the same stallion she'd seen in the Oscurita stables. It stamped down out of the painting, blinking in the bright light of La Luminosa, the jewels on its harness glittering. The Baron was dressed finely, but not armoured. He looked just like a rich diplomat coming to negotiate trade routes. The guards hesitated, stunned by the sight of the Baron emerging from a painting, and bewildered by the huge black horse standing in the Duchess's quarters.

That's just what he wants! Bianca seized the first thing that came to hand – a poker from the Duchess's fireplace.

'Traitor!' she yelled and made a run for the Baron, planning to knock him from the horse and put his lights out with the hard iron poker. But Captain Raphaeli caught her as she tried to run past him and held her tight around the shoulders. Bianca's feet skidded on the tiled floor as she writhed, trying to get out of his grip.

'Guards!' Raphaeli called. 'Seize that man!'

40

The stunned guards leapt into action. They grabbed the Baron and dragged him from the horse, throwing him to the floor. Bianca stopped struggling from pure relief.

Two guards immediately flanked the Baron, holding his arms. His horse bucked and reared, looking like it wanted to bolt – but there was nowhere in this room full of people and furniture that it could bolt to. More guards raised their spears and it whinnied in fear. Then there was a flash of red and Marco vaulted over the couch, between a pair of guards, and grabbed the horse's reins. He whispered to it and it seemed to calm down.

'I am a peaceful representative of the Duchess of Oscurita,' declared the Baron. The guards were holding his head down so he couldn't look directly at Duchess Catriona, but he spoke in a strong, clear voice. 'I am here on a visit of diplomacy.'

'Diplomacy my foot!' Bianca shouted.

'You are a traitor,' snarled Captain Raphaeli, letting go of Bianca – but taking the poker from her hand at the same time. 'You attempted to kill the Duchess, and you *will* be punished for it.'

'Master Filpepi, the artist, was the true mastermind of that foul plot,' said the Baron.

In the corner of the room, Bianca saw Lucia and Cosimo give each other pale, miserable looks. Cosimo took Lucia's hand, and Bianca was quite glad. Lucia might be a pain, but it wasn't her fault her old master had been a traitor. She had known nothing of Filpepi's elaborate plan to replace Duchess Catriona with a living, painted replica of herself.

'I was a loyal citizen until Filpepi drew me into his schemes,' the Baron went on. 'I was merely a pawn . . . just as the Duchess herself was.'

Bianca felt her face flush hot and red at the pure cheek of it. 'You liar!' she shouted. 'I know exactly who was behind the plot – Edita of Oscurita! You plotted to murder the Duchess, and you killed Annunzio di Lombardi – don't pretend you didn't.'

'Be *quiet*, girl,' snapped Secretary Franco. 'Do not make me tell you again.'

'I am willing to face the full consequences of my actions in La Luminosa,' said the Baron. 'But I am here first to broker a peaceful friendship between our two cities. When my task is done I will be your prisoner and throw myself on your bountiful mercy.'

Bianca stifled a bitter laugh. Duchess Catriona was a great ruler and a good person, but she wouldn't bet on her 'bountiful mercy', not for the man who'd tried to steal her throne.

'Please,' said the Baron, 'allow me to address the Duchess, whom I have wronged so sorely.'

Captain Raphaeli glanced at Duchess Catriona and Secretary Franco. A silent conversation seemed to take place between them. Raphaeli shook his head, counselling her to refuse. Catriona looked to Franco uncertainly, pursing her lips. Franco tilted his head thoughtfully and then nodded.

Bianca caught Marco's eye and they couldn't help but smile. They had waited so long for the Baron to get his comeuppance. *She's going to lock the Baron up and throw away the key.*

The Duchess brushed down her gown and raised her chin. 'I will hear what the Baron has to say.'

Bianca's jaw dropped. The horse's reins slipped out of Marco's hands and he had to quickly snatch them up again.

I don't . . . I can't . . . What is she thinking?

'The traitor Baron da Russo will be brought before me in the throne room,' Catriona finished, then swept out of the room with Secretary Franco and half the guards hurrying in her wake. The rest of the guards dragged the Baron to his feet. As soon as she was out of sight they frogmarched him to the door, one of them taking the reins from Marco and leading his horse after them.

Bianca stood still and stared at the doorway, speechless.

Granting an audience to the Baron da Russo in the throne room? That wasn't the Duchess Bianca knew!

Chapter Five

Bianca and Marco both moved to follow the Duchess, but then Bianca hesitated, glancing at the spilled chalk and the scattered papers. She met Lucia's eyes, and Lucia gave a deep sigh.

'Oh for God's sake, don't just stand there. *Go*,' she said, waving Bianca away with both hands. 'But don't think you're not going to have plenty of chores to make up for this later!'

'Yes, Mistress Lucia, thank you!' Bianca gave her a bobbed curtsey and a bright, genuine smile, then hitched up her grey Oscuritan servant's skirts to run after the strange procession making its way to the throne room.

By the time they got there, a crowd had gathered. Bianca and Marco had to weave between the courtiers and guards to get to the foot of the steps to the throne.

Duchess Catriona had already taken her seat on the throne of La Luminosa. As Bianca looked up at Catriona's regal poise and stern, piercing glare, she quickly understood Catriona's decision to allow the Baron to speak to her here – in this room Catriona was the undisputed ruler. Captain Raphaeli marched the Baron forwards and threw him to the floor at her feet. With her official sceptre in hand and the golden sun symbol on the throne framing her head, there was no question which one of them was in charge.

The Baron tried to rise to his feet, but Captain Raphaeli firmly prodded him back to his knees. Da Russo paused to catch his breath before he spoke, and Bianca wondered if he was thinking of his time as regent, before Duchess Catriona came of age. Protocol meant he'd never sat on the actual throne, himself – but he would have, if his plan had gone as he'd hoped.

'Your Royal Highness,' he said, his voice calm and formal. 'I have come from the court of Her Highness Duchess Edita of Oscurita – the land beyond the magical paintings, known to some as the Dark City.'

'So it's true!' one of the courtiers behind Bianca whispered to her companion. 'I never believed it . . .' Bianca saw several of the lords and ladies in the crowd turn to each other, hiding their muttering behind their hands or beautiful jewel-coloured silk fans. She guessed they were mostly saying the same thing.

'They all believe you now,' Marco said under his breath. Bianca nodded, though it wasn't a lot of comfort at this moment.

'I have come as a diplomat, to offer the friendship of Oscurita, and her own, personal friendship to you, Your Highness,' the Baron went on. 'Duchess Edita wishes to reignite the intentions of your great father, the Duke, and begin an exchange of cultures between our cities. The citizens of Oscurita and La Luminosa have been separated for too long – and there will be much to trade between them.'

Bianca heard a couple of lords make interested noises under their breath and winced. *He knows there are a few greedy courtiers here who'll do almost anything to open new trade routes . . .*

Duchess Catriona nodded slowly. 'Baron da Russo,' she said in a clear, confident voice. 'Your Duchess risks much by sending you here. You are a traitor and a scoundrel, and an attempted murderer. You *will* be punished for your crimes.' Bianca's heart swelled and she felt her fists start to unclench. But Catriona wasn't finished. 'Our Royal Court is open to receiving the chosen emissaries of Her Highness Duchess Edita,' she said, and Bianca's heart sank again.

She gave Marco an outraged glare, and mouthed 'What is she *doing*?' Marco shook his head and shrugged.

'We will not turn away offers of true and peaceful friendship. *However*,' Catriona added, 'I do not mean that such offers will be accepted without due consideration. Return to Oscurita and relay my message to Duchess Edita, and convey to her my sincerest compliments. I, too, hope that our cities can coexist in harmony.'

The Baron managed to bow even though he was already on his knees. He got to his feet and turned to go.

'Captain Raphaeli,' said Duchess Catriona, 'please *escort* the Baron back to an appropriate painting.' Bianca shuddered at the reminder that any painting could be a portal to Oscurita now. Edita's forces could come through anywhere in the city, with no warning. She shook her head again, totally perplexed at the Duchess's decision to just let the Baron go. They were in so much danger, but it seemed as though Bianca was the only one to know it.

The Captain made a small signal and the Baron was instantly surrounded by guards. Although Catriona had called it an escort, it looked more like an arrest. They drew their swords and, in formation, marched him out of the room.

'Now, all of you leave me,' Duchess Catriona said, waving her sceptre at the courtiers. 'I must talk with my advisors about this development.'

The lords and ladies started to file out of the throne room, muttering to each other.

Bianca stepped forward, approaching the throne. 'Duchess, please,' she said. 'We must be –'

Duchess Catriona shifted a little in her seat and set the sceptre down on the golden table at her elbow. 'Bianca, I know what you're going to say.'

'I've still got to say it. I don't know how you can even think about believing that Edita is anything but a lying, throne-stealing manipulator who plans to invade at the first chance! How could you allow the Baron da Russo to slip out of your fingers, *again*, to go back to her and tell her that you're willing to be *friends*?'

Secretary Franco planted his wrinkled hands on his hips and shook his head. 'That's it. I won't have you talk to the Duchess like this. Guards, remove this girl, *and* the harlequin!'

A few guards stepped forward, uncertainly. Marco's shoulders rolled back and he looked like he was ready to drop into a roll as soon as one of them made a grab for him.

No! Bianca thought better of saying it aloud, but she gave Duchess Catriona a pleading look. *You won't let him do this, will you?*

Duchess Catriona held up a hand, halting the guards. 'Now, Secretary Franco, you know I agree with you, but Marco Xavier and *Lady* Bianca – true heir to Oscurita – are my trusted friends. Even though it's not her place to advise me, she may speak to me however she likes. Why don't you go and make sure the Baron has been sent back?' She spoke sweetly, but she also met his eyes steadily and tapped her fingers lightly on the arm of the throne. Bianca knew it wasn't really a suggestion, and apparently so did Franco. He bowed low and left the throne room.

Marco relaxed as the guards drew back. 'Yeah, that's right, back off,' he muttered.

When Franco had gone, Duchess Catriona got up from the throne, stretched, and sank down again on the top step of the throne's raised platform. She wriggled and shifted until her stiff skirts were spread out behind her and then patted the step.

'Come, sit,' she said.

Bianca climbed the steps and sat down, and Marco sat on the step below. Bianca looked down at her own dress – she was still wearing the plain, grey servant's dress from Oscurita. She wondered if the Baron would have recognised it. Then she thought of her mother, who might still be in disguise and running from Edita's soldiers, and her shoulders sagged.

'I just don't understand,' she said. 'I know Franco thinks

diplomacy is the only grown-up way to deal with things, but what's the point of being sensible if it puts everyone in danger?'

Duchess Catriona raised an eyebrow at Bianca. 'Oh *really*, Bianca! I'm seriously disappointed if you think that's what I'm doing.'

'Huh?' said Marco, frowning.

Bianca blinked up at Catriona. 'But then . . . what *are* you doing? You sent him back to tell Edita you wanted to be friends!'

'I do,' said the Duchess. 'Bianca, I want La Luminosa to be friends with Oscurita, more than anything! And I expect we shall be . . . as soon as your mother has taken back the city.' Her face broke into a grin that made Bianca's heart soar – it was the dangerous kind of grin that usually came just before one of the Duchess's particularly clever tricks. 'Just because I'm prepared to allow them into the city, that doesn't mean I don't expect Edita and the Baron to betray us.'

Bianca gave a huge sigh of relief to see the Duchess she recognised in front of her once more. 'So you don't really believe she wants peace?'

'Bianca, she stole your mother's throne. And she might have been behind the Baron's attempt to take mine, too! I don't trust her not to try to invade, or put some kind of puppet ruler in place here.'

Bianca felt like she'd been carrying a stack of heavy canvases and someone had taken the burden from her.

'But Secretary Franco is right about some things, you know, and he's right about this – if we can prevent war with Edita, we should try. Even if she does seem to think we're simpletons,' she added. 'That *ridiculous* horse! Did she think we'd all be so impressed with a sparkly saddle that we'd forget all you'd told us? He looked like he was going to the carnival, not bringing a serious diplomatic message.'

'And . . . if we can't prevent a war?' Marco asked.

Duchess Catriona's smile turned even more hard and cunning. 'Then we'll go to war. After all, in order to spy on us, the Baron has to be here. That means we get to watch him, too. Nobody who comes through those paintings will be alone in La Luminosa for a single second.' She gave Bianca a devious wink, and Bianca felt herself smile for what felt like the first time in days. The Duchess she knew and loved had never left her after all. Whatever the Baron brought through from the Dark City, La Luminosa would be ready for it.

Chapter Six

Bianca forced herself to walk slowly as she and Marco headed through the secret passages towards Master di Lombardi's secret workshop. Their talk with Duchess Catriona had been reassuring, but Bianca's mind was still racing off in all directions.

'What if the Duchess is wrong?' she said. 'What if letting the Baron into La Luminosa is a terrible plan? What if we lose track of him? What if this was exactly what Edita was betting on?'

'I think we should trust her,' Marco said, gently but firmly. 'There's no point dwelling on what could go wrong so much that you don't prepare for it.'

'But, what if . . .?' Bianca said, and Marco gave her a faux-stern look. 'I know, but Duchess Catriona's expecting my mother to take back the throne. What if she can't do it on her own? What if she needs our help?'

An even worse possibility lurked at the back of Bianca's mind, too horrible to voice, even to Marco. What if Catriona waited too long and Edita captured Bianca's mother first? What if she . . .?

Bianca rubbed her eyes, trying to banish the image of Duchess Edita presiding over an Oscuritan execution.

'Look,' Marco said, 'let's follow Captain Raphaeli's example – go with it, but be prepared to act if we have to.'

'Yeah, you're right.' Bianca shook off the horrible vision and smiled at Marco. 'Thanks.'

A young woman's voice echoed down the passage, stopping Bianca in her tracks.

'All right, let's put the spare springs down over there for the moment. Then we can get at whatever this is . . .'

That was Lucia's voice. And a second later, Bianca heard a chorus of other young voices answering her.

'What's she doing in here?' she said, but she realised it was a stupid thing to say as soon as she'd said it. All the apprentices knew about the secret workshop now. It was the only way.

Marco looked a bit sheepish, but shook his head. 'What could I do? We need all the help we can get.'

'Of course,' said Bianca, waving her hand as if to brush the last few moments away. 'I didn't mean it like that.' But she knew that wasn't quite true.

They rounded a corner and found the door to the secret workshop propped open. Beyond it, the workshop seemed to be swarming with people. Bianca stood in the doorway, chewing her lip. She knew she'd allowed the other apprentices into the workshop, but that was a matter of life and death – she hadn't quite realised how she'd feel when she saw Lucia and Ezio and Gabriella strolling between the inventions and workbenches, giving appraising looks to her grandfather's secret projects. Her face flushed with irritation as Lucia picked up an ornately etched brass egg the size of her fist and tapped it on the workbench beside her, as if she could crack it open.

Marco gave Lucia a small salute as he ran over to where Sebastiano was still tinkering with the strange domed Vehicle for Travelling Underneath the Canal Surface. Bianca took a deep breath and tried to make herself smile. Despite Marco's very reasonable argument, she wished she'd never let the apprentices in. It was selfish to want to keep it for herself, but that was how she felt.

Cosimo sighed. 'It's going to take us a long time to solve all the mysteries of this place,' he said, and Bianca looked down at the floor, hoping he wouldn't read the disappointment on her face. She felt silly for it – what if something here could help her mother, or save La Luminosa? – but she did not like the idea of Cosimo and Lucia solving all the mysteries her grandfather had left behind.

'How did it go with the Baron?' Lucia asked, coming over to them with the brass egg still in her hands.

Bianca looked up and saw all the apprentices staring at her, waiting for an answer. She swallowed. 'Duchess Catriona has allowed the Baron to go back to Oscurita with a message of friendship for Edita,' she said. 'She's decided to try the diplomatic route.'

'Brave,' said Cosimo quietly.

'I think it's very sensible,' said Lucia. 'I bet the Dark City is far less of a threat than it seems.'

You haven't been there, Bianca thought. *You don't know how much of a tyrant Edita really is . . .*

'Still . . .' Lucia added. 'The *Baron*. I'd expect the Duchess to be a little harsher – he did try to steal her throne, after all.'

'I tried to tell her she couldn't trust him, but she . . .' For a moment Bianca thought about telling them all the Duchess's real plans. She looked around at the faces of her fellow apprentices. These were some of the people she trusted most in the world. But then she thought better of it.

'She wouldn't listen to me,' she finished with a frown, trying to look suitably annoyed.

'Bianca, come and see what we've found!' called Marco's voice from somewhere near the back of the enormous room.

Bianca smiled, grateful for the break in the tension, and headed over to him. Domenico followed her and she saw him give Sebastiano an excited grin as she drew closer to Marco, who was holding a long sheet of parchment paper.

He waved it cheerfully as she approached. 'I found the plans! We can get it to work, I'm sure we can!'

'We can get *what* to work?' Bianca asked. 'Did you fix the flying machine?'

Marco gave a little shudder. 'I'm not going up in that thing again, no way,' he said. 'No, the other way. *Down*.' He stood back, revealing the Vehicle for Travelling Underneath the Canal Surface with a sweeping gesture.

Bianca stepped forward and laid a hand on its gently curving brass sides, then stared up at Marco, her excitement mounting. 'You mean you figured out how the bellows connect to the fin panels?'

'They don't. They connect to a whole different pulley system, and *that* connects to both the fins and the steering,' said Marco.

Bianca slapped her head with the flat of one hand. 'Of course!'

'Wouldn't it be amazing?' Marco said, hopping down from the machine and pushing a lever. A panel in the side of the machine flipped up and Bianca could see into the cabin. It had two carved wood and leather seats, right underneath the big glass dome, and a space behind them that could just about fit another passenger or some cargo. 'Imagine it, us bobbing along under the canal. Nobody would ever know we were down there!'

A prickle of fear struck the back of Bianca's neck – all she could see was the machine sinking to the bottom of the canal and never being seen again. She shuddered.

'It's all right,' said Marco. 'It's got an emergency release. If it did get stuck or something you could just open the dome and swim to the surface.'

'You could if you could swim,' muttered Bianca.

'You can't swim?' Marco looked shocked. 'How do you live in the most watery city in the world and not be able to swim? Haven't you ever fallen in the canal?'

'No, and I never plan to!' Bianca snapped. 'I'm so glad you've got it working, Marco, really – I bet it'll be really useful if Edita invades. But I don't think anyone should test it. It just seems . . . risky.'

'*Risky?*' Marco planted his hands on his hips. 'That's rich! You were the one who dragged me into that *flying machine* without a moment's thought.'

'It was an emergency. And anyway, it's different. Falling's different from drowning.'

'Yeah, worse!'

'We haven't actually got it working yet,' Domenico cut in, probably sensing a full-scale battle about to erupt. 'And even when we do, we can't test it. There's no way to get it to the canal. It doesn't fit through the door, and I don't know how we'd lift it out of the windows up there.'

Bianca frowned. 'Think of all the inventions Master di Lombardi planned out but never built. We have books full of them. But he built this one, so he must've had a plan for eventually getting it into the canal.'

'Let's look around again,' said Marco. 'Think about it; what if we need to take the Duchess away, somewhere safe and secret? This might be the only way to travel through the city without being seen.'

Bianca nodded. 'I see your point,' she said grimly. 'All right, let's have another look. There might be something in one of the books, or another way out we haven't found.'

Bianca walked to the nearest wall and started to search along it for any sign of a hidden opening. In di Lombardi's old house she'd once found a secret compartment by running her fingers over the wall, so she tried that, but she didn't feel any sudden difference in texture or temperature. The huge, rough bricks didn't seem to be hiding anything.

Bianca was just starting to think they wouldn't find anything when she heard Sebastiano calling her name.

'Bianca, come and look at this,' he said. He was standing next to a pile of crates, staring down at the floor. She walked over and looked down, trying to see what it was about that bit of floor that had interested him. Sebastiano nudged a crate aside. 'I think there's a painting under here. It's painted right onto the floor.'

Bianca blinked. She could see it now – there was a corner of something dark and smooth-looking poking out from under one of the crates. At first she'd thought it was just a big gap between the wooden floorboards. 'Help me move the crates,' she said. Marco and Domenico hurried over and between the four of them they shifted the boxes aside. It was definitely a painting – and a rather odd one. It was a square, as long on each side as Bianca was tall. Its surface was dusty and scratched, but under the layer of dust there was a deep darkness, with a shifting, glinting light reflecting back at them.

'You found it!' she said to Sebastiano, with a grin. Sebastiano blushed a little but looked really pleased. 'This is a painting of a window onto the canal.'

'There's no handle to open it up,' said Marco, walking around the edge of the painting.

'You'll have to paint one,' Domenico said, with an eager grin at Bianca.

'On one condition.' Bianca folded her arms. 'You promise you will never make me get in that thing! Drown yourselves without me.'

'I promise,' said Marco. 'Unless it's "an emergency".'

Bianca stuck her tongue out at him, but she went to find the magical paints anyway. Master di Lombardi had a whole store of them, ready-mixed and labelled, which Cosimo and Lucia were sorting through. Lucia looked like she was going to make a fuss when Bianca asked if she could use some of the *ether*, but Cosimo handed it over with a smile.

'You shouldn't be so hard on her,' Bianca heard him whisper to Lucia. 'This all belonged to her grandfather, after all.'

Bianca didn't want to let on that she'd heard him, but she smiled to herself, touched by Cosimo's words.

She picked out some white and brown paints and sat on the floor by the painted window. It wasn't a complicated shape, but it was always tricky to paint a handle because it didn't just have to look right – she had to get the shadows and colours perfect so that when she added depth to it with the paint it would become solid.

A few minutes of intense concentration later, she looked up.

'I think I'm done,' she said. 'Careful though, the paint's still wet.'

She shifted aside as Marco wrapped his hand in his sleeve and reached down. He looked nervous, as if he didn't quite believe that his fingers would be able to slip under the solid surface of the floor and grasp the handle – but they did. He pulled, and the painted window opened up as easily as if it'd been a real doorway on oiled hinges. Bianca took a step back as a blast of cold air came up from the hole in the floor, full of the pungent smell of fish, boat oil and old rope that any true La Luminosan could identify as the scent of the canal. She could hear it, too – a definitely watery sloshing and sucking. Marco dug in his pockets and found a pebble, which he dropped into the hole. It went *plop*.

'We can roll the craft down into the water on some of the spare planks,' Domenico said, excitedly.

'Now all we have to do is *actually* get it working,' Sebastiano pointed out.

Marco grinned at Bianca. 'Thanks,' he said.

Bianca rolled her eyes. 'Of course. Now shut that door – it's giving me the creeps!' She glanced again at the underwater craft. It seemed perfectly solid and comfortable on dry land, but that was one invention of her grandfather's that she was in no hurry to test out.

Chapter Seven

Bianca crouched behind a topiary bush cut into the shape of a wading bird. She peered between the spindly stalks that formed its legs, trying not to breathe hard enough to rustle the leaves.

On the other side of the bird, the walled sculpture garden was full of courtiers – half of them dressed in the traditional bright jewel colours of La Luminosa, and the other half in deep, almost-black blues and greens and purples. The diplomatic delegation from Oscurita had arrived.

There were ten of them, men and women draped in Oscuritan finery with pale skin and dark hair, who seemed extremely uncomfortable in the La Luminosan sunlight, although it was barely a few hours after dawn and the day wasn't even shaping up to be a particularly bright one. They carried parasols of inky-black silk, which cast pools of shadow around them but probably made them feel even hotter. One or two of the palest ones had collapsed onto the stone benches dotted around the garden to catch their breath. They fanned themselves with brightly coloured fans hastily borrowed from their La Luminosan counterparts, and squinted and shaded their eyes as they tried to talk trade routes and the rules of exchange and migration.

Bianca had been listening for a little while, and it bothered her that she hadn't heard anything that sounded like treachery or plans for an invasion, even when she'd made sure to catch the delegation talking amongst themselves. She would've loved to believe that it meant they weren't planning to betray La Luminosa, but she couldn't. All it meant was that they were good at hiding it.

Still, the delegation were all here, and they weren't going to be allowed to wander off by themselves, which had to be a good thing. Every few minutes Bianca checked that the palace guards were still positioned at regular intervals around the garden's walls, their golden armour and sharp spears glinting in the sunlight and making the Oscuritans wince. It might be diplomacy, but at least it was heavily guarded diplomacy.

Bianca carefully crept along a few metres to her left, sheltering in the small gap between the hedge and the sun-warmed stone wall. A little way along the path on the other side of the bushes there was a swinging wooden seat under an arch of climbing roses. Duchess Catriona sat on the seat, dressed in one of her finest – and brightest – cream gowns. The neckline was encrusted with gold and rubies that caught the light and shimmered whenever she breathed.

At her side, on an ordinary chair, sat the Baron da Russo. Bianca's lips twisted in distaste. She hated to see him sitting so close to Duchess Catriona – it only reminded her of his horrid plan to kill her and marry a painted Duchess who had no thoughts or feelings of her own. It was a creepy, creepy thought and Bianca shuddered.

She couldn't *quite* make out what the Baron was saying. She risked sneaking a little nearer, pressing herself close up behind a statue of an angel holding a golden sword.

'Many apologies . . .' said the Baron. Bianca frowned. What was he apologising for? Not his attempt to take the Duchess's crown, she was pretty sure.

Bianca felt something tickling her foot and she looked down to find a bright green spider the size of her fist crawling over her shoe. She gave a violent, involuntary shudder and kicked out, trying to dislodge it.

Her foot connected with something hard underneath the hedge, and a very quiet voice grunted in muffled pain.

Bianca froze. Sweat prickled across the back of her neck and she held her breath. Which would be worse, she wondered, being discovered by the Oscuritans or one of the palace guards? If Franco knew she was here he'd have her thrown out of the palace, possibly from a high window . . .

Then the bushes rustled and Marco crawled into her hiding space, wriggling out from under the hedge on his stomach like a lizard. Bianca let out her gasp as a silent sigh of relief.

'How did you even fit down there?' she whispered.

'Practice.' Marco grinned back. 'Spent a long time in the false bottom of a trunk for a stage routine.'

Bianca raised her hand to her mouth, fighting the laugh that bubbled up inside her. She chewed on one finger until the feeling passed and then nodded to the bower, where the Duchess was listening to the Baron with an attentive but rather glazed smile.

'I quite understand, really,' she said. 'I would not want Duchess Edita to risk her health to come here.'

'Thank you, Your Highness. You have really grown into a very fair young woman.'

Marco glanced at Bianca and pulled a face, sticking out his tongue.

'The sunlight is simply too much for Her Highness,' the Baron went on, with an exaggerated sadness. 'She is particularly sensitive to light, and would find it difficult to visit your beautiful city even at night. However, the Duchess so sincerely wished to be here that she asked me to present you with this gift, as a symbol of the great friendship of our two cities.' He turned and beckoned, and two La Luminosan servants appeared, pushing something large and heavy on a wheeled platform. The object was as tall as a man and about twice as wide, draped in a sheet of black silk.

Duchess Catriona watched it approaching with an expression of deep and unconcealed suspicion. She looked just like Bianca felt. Bianca saw Captain Raphaeli's hand stray to the hilt of his sword. He gave the leading servant a sharp look, and she nodded. Raphaeli's hand didn't move, but he didn't draw his sword either.

The servants pulled back the silk sheet, and Bianca let out a sigh of relief – and then winced a little. The Baron's gift was a lifelike and life-size statue of Duchess Edita embracing Duchess Catriona, carved from plain white marble. Edita seemed to have been caught in the moment of drawing Catriona into a hug – they were facing each other, and Edita's arm was around Catriona's shoulders while her other hand was raised to touch her cheek. The Edita statue's face wore an expression of perfect sweetness and affection that made Bianca shudder.

'Sickening!' she hissed to Marco. '*And* it's not even very good!'

Marco frowned at the statue. 'Looks pretty good to me.'

'Well, it's not! I could explain the technical reasons why it's not, but . . .'

Marco raised an eyebrow at Bianca. 'You sure you're not being a tiny bit childish?'

Bianca looked again at the statue and sagged. 'Yeah. Maybe. A tiny bit.'

The Baron was sitting with an expectantly smug look on his face while Duchess Catriona stood up and walked around the statue. She returned to her bower and sat down, her back regally straight. 'This is the work of Piero Filpepi, is it not?' she asked the Baron. Her voice was steady, but her stare so sharp it could've cut through stone.

Bianca pressed her lips together, afraid she might let out a gasp of recognition and they'd be caught. Of course it was Filpepi's work!

For a second, the Baron actually looked slightly worried. Then his expression smoothed over once more.

'I apologise for any offence, Your Highness,' he said. 'The truth is that the traitor Filpepi is currently languishing in an Oscuritan jail for his crimes against La Luminosa. We did set him to work on the statue, as he was the only Oscuritan artist capable of producing a true likeness of Your Highness. Simply say the word and we return the gift to Duchess Edita.'

Bianca saw Marco wince. 'She can't do that – his explanation's too good, it'd be an insult,' he whispered.

Duchess Catriona sat still and silent for a moment longer, then turned a thin smile on the Baron. 'Please convey my deepest thanks to Duchess Edita for her thoughtful and touching gift,' she said. 'I shall cherish it.'

Bianca sincerely hoped that 'cherish it' was secret code for 'throw it into the canal as soon as your back is turned', but she did feel proud of Catriona for keeping up the façade of politeness.

'Tell me, Baron,' said the Duchess. 'How is it that you were able to stand living in La Luminosa for so long? Nobody ever suspected that you weren't one of us,' she added, without bothering to hide the bitterness in her voice. 'Doesn't the light bother you?'

'In fact,' said the Baron, 'I've always been perfectly comfortable in La Luminosa. Although I was raised in Oscurita, I am half Luminosan by blood. My father was a Luminosan lord who crossed over into Oscurita back when the ways between our cities were not widely known.'

Bianca pulled a face. The Baron had a Luminosan father and Oscuritan mother? That was far too much like her own story for her taste.

'I understand that the dark of Oscurita is as difficult for us as the light of La Luminosa is for Oscuritans,' said Duchess Catriona, her bitterness fading as she leaned forwards a little in genuine interest. 'It must be hard for a couple to fall in love when they can't stand to live in each other's worlds.' Bianca knew it was very hard. She thought again of her own parents, separated by magic and war and the limitations of their own bodies.

'In fact, that's not always the case,' said the Baron. 'I believe that enough children have been born of mixed parentage over the years that some people do have a latent ability to cope. My father could live comfortably in Oscurita, though I remember him carrying a lamp wherever he went. And His Highness, Duke Annunzio di Lombardi . . .'

'May he rest in peace,' Catriona added pointedly.

'May he rest in peace,' echoed the Baron. 'As you know, he was able to live in La Luminosa for more than a decade, although his tolerance for the light wasn't passed on to either of his daughters.'

'How much did my father know about all this?' Duchess Catriona asked. 'He never mentioned it to me – but I must have been only three or four when the ways between our cities were closed.'

'Oh, he knew all about Oscurita,' said the Baron. 'In fact . . . I suppose you never knew, as it never came to pass, but there was once talk of an allegiance between our two worlds, formalised by marriage.'

'Marriage?' Duchess Catriona drew herself up in surprise and the seat underneath her swayed slightly on its thick chains. 'Who was to marry who?'

'It was two years after you were born, Your Highness,' said the Baron. 'Your mother the Duchess was dead two years and your father was considering remarriage. A union between the royal families would have been politically astute and might have helped him recover from his grief.'

Duchess Catriona's face turned pale. 'I . . . I never knew,' she said. 'Nobody ever told me! Surely the older courtiers and the servants must remember this?'

The Baron shook his head. 'Duke Annunzio led a delegation to La Luminosa in secret. He presented himself to the court as master artist and brought his eldest daughter, the Princess Saralinda, in disguise as a simple apprentice. Your father was the only one who knew the truth – he and Saralinda met and talked together several times.'

Bianca suddenly felt as if the earth under her feet was rocking back and forth. She had to grab on to one of the angel's wings to steady herself. Her mother . . . and Catriona's father . . .

'Of course, that was shortly before poor Princess Saralinda's tragic descent into insanity,' the Baron added, with such a look of genuine sadness that Bianca's faintness fled instantly. She trembled with the urge to leap from behind the hedge and punch him in the face. Marco grabbed her wrist and she realised she had actually made a fist and drawn it back. She dropped her shoulders and stared at him, feeling the blood draining and rushing back to her face in a constant cycle of shock and wonder.

'It's OK. We'll find out if it's true,' Marco whispered. 'I promise.'

Bianca gave him a tight, bewildered smile and nodded, grateful to know he was thinking exactly what she was thinking.

Was it possible she and Duchess Catriona were half-sisters?

Chapter Eight

'Your Highness,' came Secretary Franco's voice. Bianca peered around the stone angel's right wing to see him walking down the garden path towards Duchess Catriona in her rose-covered archway. He was leaning on a golden staff and still wearing his bright sunflower-yellow robes. Several of the Oscuritan lords and ladies shied away from him as he passed. He came to Duchess Catriona's side and bowed deeply. 'Midday approaches, and I believe our Oscuritan guests would like to retire to their rooms for an hour before lunch is served.'

Bianca saw a few of the Oscuritans nod, while the rest looked like they desperately wanted to but were still trying to act as if the light and heat of the day wasn't bothering them.

'Then let us go in,' said Duchess Catriona, getting to her feet. 'We have achieved plenty for our first morning. I have . . . much to consider.'

The Oscuritans started to gather their fans and parasols and to make a hasty beeline for the doors to the palace. Though she was still in shock, Bianca couldn't help but smile at the sight of the Luminosan courtiers strolling after them with slow, smug steps.

'May I ask a favour, Your Highness?' said the Baron. 'As I am not of the same delicate constitution as my compatriots, may I have your permission to take my leave from you to visit some of my favourite places in La Luminosa? I called this beautiful city home for so many years, I would love to be able to explore it once more.'

You lost the right to explore La Luminosa when you tried to steal it! Bianca thought angrily.

Duchess Catriona's brows drew down, and for a moment Bianca thought she was going to say something along those lines. But then Secretary Franco bent down and said something to her, something Bianca couldn't make out. Catriona listened, without taking her eyes off the Baron, and then smiled.

'Thank you, Secretary Franco. Baron, you may take a walk through La Luminosa. I can only imagine how much you must have missed it.'

'Thank you very much, Your Highness,' said the Baron, smiling greasily and bowing.

'And my guards will keep a comfortable distance as they accompany you,' said Duchess Catriona, 'so you can reminisce in peace.'

The Baron straightened up, still smiling, though the smile was frozen on his face. 'I appreciate it,' he said, through gritted teeth.

'He's up to no good,' Marco whispered to Bianca.

'I can't believe he thought the Duchess would let him wander off on his own,' Bianca muttered back. 'He obviously wanted to do something . . . without anyone . . .' She trailed off, an idea sparking in the back of her mind. Could it be so simple to discover what he was up to?

Marco nudged her and raised his eyebrows. Bianca looked back at him and smiled, then began to hurry back along behind the hedges at a hopping run, Marco on her heels.

Captain Raphaeli was in his office in the palace's guard barracks, examining a stack of papers. He looked up when Bianca and Marco burst in and immediately leapt to his feet, his hand going to the hilt of his sword.

'What's happened? Is the Duchess all right?'

'She's fine! She's brilliant! I've got a plan,' Bianca gasped.

'Slow down.' Raphaeli folded his arms. 'Bianca, I know you mean well, but I can't have you running in here like this.'

'But I know how we can find out what the Baron's planning to do,' said Bianca. 'The Duchess is letting him go for a walk around the city – heavily guarded, obviously.'

'I know, I've already assigned the guards. They won't let him out of their sight, I promise.'

'That's just it, I want them to!' Bianca said. Captain Raphaeli gave her a sceptical look, but didn't immediately tell her she was crazy. She took this as a good sign and barrelled on. 'If he thinks he's given the guards the slip, he'll go right to wherever he wants to go,' Bianca explained. 'But Marco and I will follow him. We can blend in and hide more easily than the guards. He won't see us.'

Captain Raphaeli looked from Bianca to Marco, and frowned. 'This is a huge responsibility, you know. If you lose him, you could be endangering the Duchess – and the whole city.'

'I know,' said Bianca. 'I promise. But it could be the only way to find out what he's really after.'

'We know the streets inside out,' Marco added.

'And we can use the passages if we need to hide or something!' Bianca said.

Captain Raphaeli hesitated, deep in thought. 'I can station guards in civilian clothes around the city,' he said. 'They'll keep an eye on you and make sure the Baron doesn't vanish. You can report anything suspicious you see him do to them.'

Bianca resisted the urge to shriek with joy. 'We will,' she said. 'I swear. You just need to tell the guards to let him slip away and we'll do the rest.'

Raphaeli's stern face cracked into a smile. 'You're quite the strategist, aren't you?'

Bianca beamed at him.

The Baron da Russo strolled beside the canals, wandered down the grand roadways and slipped through the narrow alleyways of La Luminosa, and Bianca and Marco followed his every move. He'd given his guards the slip when he'd gone into a tailor's shop and they had let him leave through the back door, but Marco and Bianca had been hiding behind a table stacked with rolls of fabric and carved bone buttons.

Bianca had expected that he would head straight for some dingy parlour where he'd meet his secret accomplices, or perhaps he'd hide in plain sight, casually dropping some message into a hiding place in the Piazza del Fiero. They passed through the Piazza del Fiero, but the Baron did nothing apart from pausing to smile up at the cat-sized statues of firebreathing dragons that lined the roof of one of the houses and taking a deep sniff at a stall selling spiced apple cakes.

'So . . .' Marco said, while they were far enough away from the Baron to have a conversation without him hearing them, 'what do you think? Could your father really be the old Duke of La Luminosa?'

'I don't know,' Bianca said, 'but I suppose it must have been someone my mother met and fell in love with when she visited La Luminosa.' Bianca hesitated, sending up a brief prayer. *Please let her be all right.* 'Perhaps it was someone else at court – one of the other courtiers or something.'

Marco gave Bianca an intense look and Bianca drew back. 'What?'

'Just trying to see if I can think of any courtiers that look a bit like you,' he said. A mischievous light glinted in his eyes. 'What if your father is Secretary Franco?'

Bianca gasped and gave Marco a playful, but quite hard, punch on the arm. 'I'm nothing like Franco! Shut up and watch the Baron.'

She didn't really need to remind Marco – the Baron was walking at a gentle pace just a little way ahead and hadn't done anything remotely suspicious.

'Oh God, I don't look like Franco, do I?'

Marco rolled his eyes at her.

'Good.'

They followed the Baron all the way to the Museum of Art and trailed him from painting to statue to painting. Bianca revised her guess – she was sure he was looking for a particular painting. He would do something to it, leave some signal to tell the Oscuritan soldiers which painting to invade through. But he didn't try to touch any of the paintings. He didn't do anything except sit on one of the marble benches at the feet of the giant statue of Grand Duchess Angelica that loomed in the centre of the great hall, and look around as if he really had missed the sight of all these works of art.

'I didn't think he cared so much about art,' Marco muttered, peering around the Grand Duchess's skirts.

But Bianca's thoughts were elsewhere. 'You know, my mother was supposed to be thinking about marrying the Duke,' she whispered. 'They spent all that time together. It does seem the most logical choice.'

'But then they didn't get married,' Marco reminded her. 'Don't you think they would have, if they'd found out she was having a baby? You.'

'Maybe he didn't know until it was too late and Edita had captured her! Maybe Duchess Catriona and I really are sisters.' Bianca found herself smiling at the thought. It was huge, and terrifying . . . and yet there certainly wasn't anyone she'd rather have as a big sister than Catriona. 'Wouldn't that be great?'

Marco didn't answer. He pulled a face, and then stepped away from her before she could ask what the face had meant. The Baron had stood up, and they followed him out of the museum. He walked for about twenty more minutes before suddenly turning back towards the palace. Bianca and Marco dodged into a doorway and pretended to be very interested in a piece of scrawled graffiti they found there. When the Baron had passed them by, Bianca let out a frustrated groan.

'There's *no way* he's really just sightseeing,' she said. 'There's got to be *something*!'

'Come on.' Marco linked his arm through hers and they set off after the Baron again.

He crossed the Grand Canal at the Bridge of Cats, and Marco and Bianca paused, half-hidden behind one of the big black marble panthers that reared up on either side of the bridge, watching the Baron as he strolled to the middle and then leaned over and looked into the water.

Whatever he had slipped away for, he'd either done it without them noticing or he wasn't going to do it at all. Bianca felt almost worse than if they'd lost track of him.

'Do you think he knows we're following him?' Marco muttered.

'Why don't you think it'd be good if Catriona and I were related?' Bianca asked Marco.

Marco sighed. 'It's just . . . I don't know if the Duchess would be all that pleased to have to share La Luminosa with a long-lost baby sister,' he said.

'But it's not just some interloper, it's me,' Bianca pointed out. 'We're friends.'

'Still. Catriona thinks of the city as hers. Just hers. And . . . I think she feels the same way about her father.'

Bianca frowned and absent-mindedly reached out to stroke one of the feral cats that lay sunning themselves on the bridge's balustrades. She remembered the shocked look on Catriona's face when the Baron had revealed that her father had thought of remarrying.

'I hadn't thought of that,' she said.

'Anyway, think of all the extra princessing you'd have to do if you were royalty in Oscurita *and* La Luminosa,' Marco said. 'You couldn't run around spying on traitors with me. You'd have to sit and have polite conversation with them instead. You'd have to listen to Secretary Franco all the time!'

'Ugh.' Bianca gave an exaggerated shudder. 'No thanks.'

Suddenly, Marco seized her arm.

'What?' Bianca asked, but Marco put his finger to his lips and pointed to the canal. Bianca turned just in time to see ripples spreading through the water in a perfect circle, starting from right below where the Baron was standing. 'What was it?' Bianca whispered.

'I'm not sure,' said Marco. 'But I'm sure I saw him drop something in – and not by accident either. He leaned over and let it go.'

Bianca watched the ripples. They seemed to be larger and go on for longer than she would expect, but as soon as she'd thought that, they smoothed out and vanished.

'What was it?' Bianca repeated. 'Why would he drop something in the canal?'

The Baron was moving off again, making for the palace with a spring in his step that Bianca did not like one bit. She stepped around the marble panther onto the bridge and, as quickly as she dared without catching up to the Baron, walked up to the spot the Baron had just left.

Bianca stared down over the parapet of the bridge, but the ripples were gone, and the canal was deep and dark.

'What are we going to tell the Captain?' Marco asked, drawing level with her. 'We can't exactly rally the troops because we spotted the Baron littering.'

Bianca turned and watched the Baron da Russo as he started to climb the worn steps that led up from the side of the Grand Canal to the main gate of the palace.

'I don't know,' she said. 'But whatever it was he dropped, I somehow don't think we've seen the last of it.'

Chapter Nine

Bianca put down her paintbrush, looked up at the bright Luminosan stars glittering through the secret workshop's high windows, and sighed. She and Marco had reported back to Raphaeli about what they had seen when tailing the Baron, but the Captain was just as stumped as they were. Without any more leads, Bianca had agreed to get on with some commissions – hopefully focusing her mind would allow some answers to come to her.

Bianca looked round at her grandfather's cluttered studio, now packed with apprentice artists. Cosimo and Lucia had decided that the equipment in di Lombardi's private refuge was so much better than Filpepi's that it would be silly to go on working in their old studio. Some of the apprentices were still in the studio, but a few paintings and the small clay sculpture of a pair of dancers that Rosa was working on had been moved across to the secret workshop, and Cosimo and Lucia themselves were still sorting through the notes and tools and mysterious inventions.

Bianca smiled as her gaze set upon Marco, flat on his back, peering curiously at the underside of the underwater steam cart – despite Lucia pointing out that he was a tumbler, not an artist, or a mechanic. Bianca suspected he wouldn't leave unless Lucia physically picked him up and carried him out of the door.

Bianca had wanted to continue searching the studio for inventions and recipes that might be useful when Oscurita finally attacked, but Lucia had pointed out that if the Oscuritans didn't invade then Lady Stellata, an influential – and argumentative – aristocrat, would want to know where her commission was. Cosimo had also said, rather more gently, that it couldn't hurt for Bianca to do something normal, just for a few hours.

The evening was wearing on, but she didn't like the idea of going to bed – everything was too unresolved and she felt as if she'd achieved exactly nothing except create more questions.

She looked down at the Stellata commission she was working on – an intricate painting of a tree with a different bird perched on every branch. When it was finished, the birds would flap their wings and puff up their chests as if they were alive. Bianca was working on the trunk of the tree, adding rough bark and knots and the occasional tiny insect or sprig of moss.

It was important, intricate work and she knew she should've been happy to be trusted with it, even though she was working almost exclusively with shades of brown. But another thought kept pushing to the front of her mind, elbowing aside anything else she tried to concentrate on.

'I think I ought to go back to Oscurita,' she said aloud, breaking the silence in the studio. She turned around on her stool to face the others.

Rosa looked up from shaving paper-thin slivers of clay off the frock coat of one of the dancers. Her expression was kind, but she shook her head. 'I don't think it'll help for you to go back there, Bianca.'

'I need to talk to my mother,' Bianca said. 'I can't just sit here not knowing if she's all right, not knowing . . . anything about my father.' She stopped herself from saying 'not knowing if my father is the Duke of La Luminosa'.

'Your mother gave you a pretty specific instruction, though, didn't she?' said Marco.

Bianca deflated. 'Yes. She made me promise not to go back unless I had no other option.'

'There you go, then,' said Lucia briskly.

'Isn't there another way you can contact her?' Marco said slowly, and Bianca saw Lucia roll her eyes. 'Didn't Edita manage to talk to you through a painting, before?'

'That's right,' Bianca said, brightening. 'I was drawing her portrait and it came to life and spoke to me.' Her face fell again. 'I don't know how it was done, though.'

'Well,' said Lucia, snatching up a blank canvas from a pile by her side, 'if you're going to do it, then do it. Don't sit there moping about it.' She swapped the blank canvas for the bird painting, and shook her head when Bianca turned a grateful smile on her. 'I'd rather save the work for an apprentice who can concentrate properly,' she said. 'Hurry up and talk to your mother.'

'I'll try,' said Bianca.

She seized a palette, a stick of sketching charcoal, and a whole armful of different magical paints from the cupboard of painting supplies. Cosimo sighed and made a mark against the ones she'd taken on the inventory list he was making.

Bianca sat in front of the blank canvas and tried to see the drawing in front of her. It was a strategy di Lombardi had taught her, almost more like a meditation than a painting technique. The point wasn't to decide where every line was going to go – it was to convince yourself that there was a completed picture buried under the surface of the stiff white fabric, and all you had to do was find it.

Bianca tried to see her mother on the canvas, as if it was a mirror and Saralinda was standing just behind her shoulder.

She reached out with her hand and began to sketch, very lightly, tracing the lines of her mother's face that swam in and out of focus in front of her. The expression Bianca had seen on Saralinda's face most often was either soft-eyed love or grim determination, but for some reason she now found herself drawing Saralinda's eyes shut and her head slightly tilted, as if she was dozing peacefully.

Bianca kept adding detail to the portrait, hoping that whatever Edita had done to contact her through her painting, Saralinda would be able to do the same.

Bianca forced herself to stop fiddling with the shading on Saralinda's cheek, knowing that if she touched it any more she would add something that would hurt the picture, not make it better. She very deliberately put down her charcoal stick and picked up di Lombardi's paintbrush, holding it gently in front of her and staring at the various magical paints she'd laid out on the table beside her.

There were some she could use in her sleep: *animare* for

basic movement, *respirare* to give the illusion of regular breathing, *ether* to add space, *shimmer* and *glimmer* and *luce stellare* for different kinds of light, *saltatio* to make the subject of a painting dance.

There were a few others she wasn't so sure of. She guessed a *profumo* would add a scent to a painting, but didn't know how to use it. There was a *riflettere*, too, which looked like a jar full of liquid mirror. And finally, she had taken a vial of the precious, pure *lux aurumque* – the pure oil of the glowing golden flowers that only grew in Oscurita.

Bianca used the *ether*, then the *respirare*, until her drawing of Saralinda seemed to stand out from the canvas, breathing deeply. She added some *animare* to make Saralinda's head move slightly as she breathed, and then . . .

Nothing.

Bianca was stumped. She had no idea how to use the picture to communicate with Oscurita.

Lucia came over. 'That's a wonderful sketch,' she said. 'Now, please, give me the paints so we can all get on with our work?'

'I'm not finished,' Bianca said. 'Please, just a little longer.'

'What are you going to do?' Lucia asked pointedly.

'I . . . I . . .' Bianca seized the vial of *lux aurumque*. 'I don't know, but I can't just give up.'

'Come on, that's enough now,' said Lucia. She grabbed several of the other paints from the table, but Bianca didn't care. She was going to have to make the paint for this herself. She just didn't know how.

'Please don't waste the *lux aurumque*, Bianca,' said

Cosimo gently. 'We still don't know exactly where we're going to get more from.'

'If you'd let me go to Oscurita I could've brought you some back,' Bianca said, a little childishly.

'Don't you have something of hers you could use as an ingredient?' Lucia asked. 'Perhaps that would make a connection between her and you.'

Bianca turned to blink at Lucia in surprise. That was a good, genuinely helpful, idea!

'Well, if you're not going to let us get on with our work, we might as well try and help,' she said, rolling her eyes. '*Do* you have anything that belongs to your mother?'

Bianca thought of the medallion that opened the passages between Oscurita and La Luminosa – her mother's gift to her as a baby, which she'd let Edita trick her into handing over.

'No, nothing,' she said.

Lucia gave an exasperated sigh. 'What about *you*? You're her daughter; your blood is her blood, right? Would you prick yourself with a needle?'

Rosa looked uneasy. 'Are you sure you want to mess with that stuff without knowing what you're doing?'

Marco's head suddenly popped up through the door of the underwater machine, like a rabbit sticking its head out of its warren. 'You've used your hair before, remember? In the recipe di Lombardi left you!'

'Of course!' Bianca remembered the *storia* recipe her grandfather had given her. When she'd painted it onto the canvas, it'd moved all by itself, forming pictures to show her the story of their escape from Oscurita during the war.

She reached up and carefully pulled a hair out of her head at the root. She thought for a second, and then flipped open the vial of *lux aurumque* and dropped the hair inside. It fizzed and sparkled, and then dissolved altogether, leaving the glowing golden liquid streaked with swirling spirals of chestnut brown.

Lucia let out a frustrated gasp. 'No, Bianca, don't contaminate it all! Are you crazy? Give me that.' She made a grab for the *lux aurumque*, but Bianca pulled it back. 'You've spoiled the whole vial! You know how many magical paints that ought to have made?' Her hand snaked out and seized Bianca's wrist, and her other hand snatched the vial, which slipped out of her fingers. Bianca made a frantic attempt to catch it, which only sent it shooting up into the air, turning over and over in a display of juggling that she certainly couldn't have managed if she'd been trying.

The artists and Marco all watched and winced as the golden oil flew out of the vial and splashed across the portrait of Saralinda. For a moment she looked like she was wearing a glowing golden mask over her eyes, and then the precious fluid sank into the canvas and vanished completely.

'Bianca, I'm going to kill you,' Lucia growled. 'I don't care what the Duchess says, you're grounded for a month. You're going to be cleaning the studio from top to bottom – *including* the sulphur pots!'

'That was not my fault, *you're* the one that chucked it in the air,' Bianca snapped.

'*You'd* already contaminated the whole vial –'

'Girls!' said Saralinda.

Bianca and Lucia both turned, slowly, to find Bianca's mother looking out at them from the charcoal drawing. She was still mostly made up of sketchy black lines, but her eyes were blue and startlingly real.

'I know this is a dream,' said Saralinda, 'but even so, don't fight over a vial of *lux aurumque*.' Bianca's hands flew to her mouth. 'When I'm Duchess again I shall plant a whole field of the flowers and send them to you in their hundreds.'

'Mother!' Bianca gasped, tears springing to her eyes. 'Is it really you?'

Saralinda looked around the room for a moment in confusion. 'Bianca? What's going on? I'm quite sure I'm asleep right now. Are you really talking to me?'

'Yes!'

'How odd,' Saralinda said. 'And who are these people?'

'This is Mistress Lucia and Master Cosimo,' Bianca said, shifting aside to let her mother see into the studio. 'They're running the art studios here, now that grandfather and Filpepi are both gone. And this is Rosa – she's Head Apprentice,' Bianca added, beckoning Rosa over. Rosa stepped up to the painting nervously, brushing at her dress and trying to pat down her gravity-defying curls.

'Good, um . . . Hello, Your Highness,' she said, bobbing a curtsey.

'Nice to meet you,' said Saralinda.

'Oh, and Marco's here,' said Bianca, as Marco climbed out of the underwater machine and hurried over. He leaned into Saralinda's line of sight and waved.

'Oh, hello, Marco! How nice to see you again.'

Marco beamed and blushed.

Cosimo put a hand on Lucia's shoulder. 'I think we should give Bianca and her mother some space to talk.'

'You're still in trouble,' Lucia muttered. Bianca beamed at her, not caring how many sulphur pots she'd have to clean.

'Are you all right? Did you get to the Resistance safely?' she asked her mother.

'I'm fine. Pietro was right, I was much less suspicious by myself. I managed to slip past the guards easily. The Resistance have been gathering supporters while I was in prison – far more than I knew. Half the city is secretly on our side and the other half will come over to us as soon as they realise we have a chance of defeating Edita.'

'Does that mean it's safe enough for me to come and see you?' Bianca asked.

Saralinda shook her head. 'Absolutely not! I can't have you putting yourself in danger, now more than ever. Promise me you won't try to come here.'

'I'll promise,' Bianca said, 'if . . .' She glanced around at the other artists and Marco. All of them had the decency to pretend not to be listening, but she knew they would hear her. She took a deep breath. She'd come this far – she had to follow through. 'If you tell me who my father really is.'

Saralinda's eyebrows shot up. 'Oh! What . . . erm . . . Right now?'

'I really need to know,' Bianca said. 'I'm sorry to do it like this but I . . . I heard something that made me think maybe I know who it is and I can't go on behaving as if I don't.' Bianca was aware of Lucia and Cosimo exchanging glances with each other. To their credit, they then moved further away, into the recesses of the enormous studio.

'You . . . You think you know?' Saralinda said. 'You mean he's . . . Did someone say something to you? Does . . . does *he* know?'

Bianca frowned. That didn't sound right. Her mother knew the old Duke was dead. 'Um – it's just something the Baron said. He was talking about La Luminosa and Oscurita and he said that you came to visit La Luminosa once. He said you'd come on a . . . diplomatic mission to see the old Duke. Catriona's father.' She tried to keep her words neutral, not wanting to say outright 'was he my father too?' but not wanting to risk being unclear either.

'Oh, Bianca!' Saralinda's oddly blue eyes lit up with understanding. 'No. I know what you're thinking. I'm so sorry you had to hear about it like that. I did meet your father on that trip. The Duke was . . . very kind. He was a good friend to me. And to your father.'

Bianca smiled. 'Thank you. But please, Mother, don't leave me guessing like this!'

Saralinda paused, deep in thought, and Bianca held her breath. In the sudden hush, Bianca heard something odd . . . It was a sound like trickling water, like the sound of rainwater the morning after a heavy storm, making its way from the roofs and gutters of La Luminosa down to the canals and the sea.

Is there a leaking sink? Bianca wondered.

'My dear Bianca, I don't even know for certain if he's still alive, let alone living in La Luminosa,' Saralinda said.

'I really think it would be a better idea for us to talk this through in person, when all . . .' She hesitated. 'What is that noise?'

'Can you hear it too? There's something dripping in here,' Bianca said, looking around to try and find the source of the sound.

'Dripping? Oh no –'

A short, piercing shriek split the air in the studio and Bianca almost fell off her stool. She looked up to see Lucia backing away from one of the easels that still held paintings di Lombardi had started and never completed. Water was dribbling slowly out from underneath the white sheet that'd been draped over the painting. Bianca searched the wall behind it and the skylight up above for any sign of a leak, but there was none. The water was coming from the easel itself.

'I'm sorry, Bianca, I have to wake up,' said Saralinda. 'I have to do something about this. I love you!'

'About what?' Bianca gasped. 'What's going on?'

But the picture had closed its eyes and stopped moving. Saralinda was gone.

Bianca watched as Rosa squared her shoulders and stepped up to the painting, tugging the white sheet off it and jumping back quickly. The painting was a street scene, with a few tall houses looming over a steep road where a pedlar sold hot coffee from a cart and children played with a pair of wooden knights on horseback. And water was pouring from the doors and windows of all the houses, trickling down the street and out of the bottom of the picture, splashing down on the wooden floor of di Lombardi's studio.

Chapter Ten

Bianca twisted the paintbrush key in the lock, tugged open the door to the secret passages and leapt through, only to yelp and almost slip when her feet splashed down in a shallow puddle of water.

'What?' she gasped, glancing up and down the passage. The painted stone floor was covered in water. It reflected the flickering light of the endlessly burning torches that lined the walls. 'What is happening?' Bianca hitched up her skirts and, after a moment's thought, slipped off her thin canvas shoes.

Marco paused in the doorway while he took his shoes off too. 'Something somewhere must have sprung a leak.'

'Should we get out of here?' Rosa asked, peering through behind them.

'Let's get back to the palace,' Cosimo agreed. 'If the passages get flooded out we could be trapped in here.'

Cosimo and Lucia led the apprentices warily into the soaking passages and through the magical door that led to their quarters in the palace. They both reluctantly agreed to let Bianca and Marco continue towards the secret entrance near the throne room to report events to the Duchess. But not before Cosimo gave Bianca a stern warning: 'Just remember your place, Bianca. Even though you might be right about the threat from Oscurita, the running of La Luminosa should be left to its Duchess – *not* an apprentice painter.'

Bianca nodded her understanding before hurrying off down the passage to the turning and looking both ways, curling her toes in the cold, slightly grubby water. 'It's all one puddle – I bet this is the same water that's leaking through the door in the painting in the studio.'

Marco pulled a face at the slightly twisted logic. 'We need to tell the Duchess quickly.'

'I plan to tell everyone!' Bianca said, splashing down the corridor, looking for the closest door that would get them into the palace. 'This could ruin every magical painting in the city! Half of them probably already have some water damage. We have to find the leak and get it closed, quick.'

She opened the door that led out into the old Duke's closed-up study, and jumped down from the painting carefully so as not to let the puddle in the passages get any closer to the door. The painted big cats in the exotic garden paced back and forth as they always did, and Bianca looked at them with her heart pounding. Could they stop this before the water reached the door of this mural and started to wash the lion and the tiger away?

The palace was quiet and dim. For Bianca, who could happily walk the dark streets of Oscurita, the golden glow of the night lamps in the corridors was more than enough light to see by, but Marco walked into a low table and nearly upset an intricate golden clock. Bianca caught it and glanced at the face. No wonder the palace was so quiet – it was past midnight. She'd lost all track of time.

'Who'll be awake at this hour?' Marco asked. 'Or who can we wake up to deal with a leak inside a painting?'

Bianca thought for a second. 'Captain Raphaeli?' she suggested. 'It might be a crime, possibly, and it's *definitely* a hazard. Plus, he's always believed our crazy ideas so far . . .'

'Good idea,' said Marco, and led the way down the gently curving steps towards the main entrance hall of the palace and the doors out to the courtyard and the barracks.

But when Bianca reached the bottom of the steps, she grabbed Marco's arm. 'Listen! Voices – coming from the throne room.' She frowned at him, trying to imagine any good reason that the throne room would be full of people at this hour.

They hurried along the corridor, their still-wet feet slapping on the tiled floor, until the throne room came into view. Bright light spilled out into the corridor and the sound of raised, worried voices grew louder.

The guards gave Bianca's slightly wet dress an odd look, but still nodded her and Marco through. Bianca strode into the room, saw the Duchess, Secretary Franco, Captain Raphaeli and a handful of other advisors and courtiers standing around looking concerned but unharmed, and let out a sigh of relief. 'Duchess, you're awake! I'm so glad. Have you seen any of the flooding?'

'Do you know what caused it?' Marco asked, glancing up at Secretary Franco.

Duchess Catriona gave Bianca a frustrated, confused look. 'What? What flooding?'

'The water! It's damaging the paintings. I don't know where it's coming from!'

'Bianca,' Catriona said, with a stern frown, 'I'm not really worried about a leak right now!'

'But there is water in the passages,' Bianca said. 'It's almost ankle deep. If we don't do something soon, the water's going to reach even more of the doors and hundreds of paintings could be ruined!'

'You – you burst in,' Secretary Franco said slowly, 'to the throne room of La Luminosa, in the middle of the night, and demand that the Duchess do something about some paintings getting wet? Am I correct?'

It did sound a bit silly when he put it like that. 'I wouldn't say demand,' Bianca said. 'I'm just saying . . . we saw the flood so we came right here.'

'With no thought for proper protocol!' snapped Franco.

'But . . . the paintings are important,' said Bianca.

Franco threw up his arms in frustration.

'They are!' shouted Bianca. With every second, more damage was done.

'Bianca, the Baron is gone,' Duchess Catriona said.

Bianca blinked. 'Gone? Escaped?'

'Vanished,' said Captain Raphaeli, glowering at nobody in particular. 'In the middle of the night. Him and the entire Oscuritan delegation. They were under heavy guard. We had removed all the magical paintings from their rooms, so they wouldn't be able to slip back without us knowing.

But when a guard checked their rooms tonight they found a charcoal outline of a door drawn on the wall, hidden behind a curtain.'

'You let them have charcoal?' Bianca said. 'But that's how they escaped last time!'

'We searched them,' Captain Raphaeli said firmly. 'But they must have smuggled some in somehow.'

'Indeed. So, I'm sorry, but this . . . whatever it is with the paintings can wait, Bianca,' said Duchess Catriona.

'Oh!' Bianca's mouth dropped open. 'I bet they're connected! I bet that flooding the passages is part of his plan!'

'Guards,' said Secretary Franco, without any malice in his voice. 'Please remove these children and escort them back to their own beds. They've already heard more than they should.'

'There's no need for that, Secretary Franco,' Duchess Catriona said.

'Yes,' Franco said to the two guards, who'd stepped forwards and were hovering behind Bianca and Marco, trying not to look uncertain, 'there is a need. Please, take hold of them and take them out of the palace.'

Bianca tried to dodge away but she didn't move fast enough – the guard closest to her seized her by the arms. Bianca wriggled and tried to break his grip, but he held firm. Marco's guard made a grab for him but he had an acrobat's reflexes and dived out of the way.

Franco's veneer of calm broke, and he dropped his head into his hands. 'Your Highness, if you allow this girl to remain here, wittering about preserving paintings at a time like this, you'll seem a fool – no, you'll *be* a fool. Bianca seems to think saving a few scribbles is more important than preventing a war. I won't stand by and let her cloud your judgement.'

'Bianca,' said Duchess Catriona, 'you know I care about the paintings, but there's something much more serious going on right now. It's the Baron! I'd have thought you'd want us to have all our attention on finding him and stopping whatever it is he's doing?'

'I'm telling you, I think they're connected!' Bianca complained, planting her bare feet on the floor and refusing to be dragged away. On the other side of the room, Marco feinted to the left and then stepped to the right.

'Come here, you . . .' said his guard, and then suddenly his feet slipped out from under him and he fell on his back in a painful-sounding clang and clank of armour. 'What the . . .?' The guard reached back to push himself up, and his hand came away from the floor wet.

'Look!' Bianca said, pointing at the painting just above where the guard had slipped. It was a scene of Santa Emilia looking at the stars through her faraway glass. Behind Emilia there was a door, and flowing under the door was a steady stream of dirty water. It dripped and dribbled down the wall, leading to a visibly spreading pool of nasty brownish water on the floor.

Bianca's guard dropped her arms. Secretary Franco's wrinkled face went slack. He looked like he was going to have a fit.

'It's all of them,' said Captain Raphaeli, turning to look

around the room. Every painting was leaking now, water streaming from the edges and corners of the paintings.

Duchess Catriona turned to Bianca, a slightly panicky look in her eyes. 'I'm sorry, Bianca,' she said. 'I should have listened –'

There was a sound like fabric ripping and Bianca looked up just in time to jump back out of the way of the tide of brown water that came crashing out of one of the paintings. It swept across the floor and soaked the feet of several of the Duchess's advisors. Duchess Catriona herself hitched up her skirts and quickly climbed the steps to stand beside the throne on its raised platform. Bianca stared, open mouthed, as she saw right through the painting and into the magical passage beyond. The water was several inches deep and flowing fast.

Bianca was too worried to say 'I told you so', but she caught Secretary Franco's eye as he looked up from the soggy, ruined edges of his sunshine-yellow robe, and shrugged.

The meeting was quickly relocated upstairs, to the small council chambers near the Duchess's secretaries' offices. The leaking paintings in the council chambers had been caught quickly and removed, and were now sitting out in the courtyard in a growing stack of wet art. It was so upsetting to see the colours beginning to run and pool in brown puddles under the canvases that Bianca had stopped and tried to tilt and stack them so that the water didn't do so much damage as it ran out. It was a losing battle, though, and Marco had had to drag her away. He'd given her a hug, and then left the palace to find his father's harlequin troupe.

The council chambers were probably the driest rooms in the palace, but even here the woven rug on the floor squished underfoot.

'Right,' said Duchess Catriona as she settled into a chair at the head of the council table. She was surrounded by guards who stood around her like a solid semi-circle of flesh and metal, and Captain Raphaeli stood by the door to the room, glaring at anyone who dared approach. 'My first act of this emergency session is this: Lady Bianca di Lombardi of Oscurita is now my official advisor on matters of art and magic.' She gave Secretary Franco a piercing look as she said this, and then tilted her head as if waiting to see if any of the courtiers or advisors would argue back. None of them did, and Bianca stifled a smile. At least whatever happened now, Franco wouldn't have any excuse to try to throw her out again.

A long parade of advisors, secretaries and servants began to file in, and Bianca sat with the Duchess and listened to their reports of the destruction, desperately trying to think of some way of sealing the passages just for now, or finding out where the water was coming from.

'The palace is full of water and mud, Your Highness,' the Chief Housekeeper, Mistress Paganini, sighed, wringing her wet cap between her hands as if she felt personally responsible for the mess. 'Every able body we have is up and working. We have a bucket chain bailing out water from the throne room and every painting that can be moved to the courtyard will be soon.'

'You must lay them down properly!' Bianca said, her heart twisting at the thought of the paintings being piled up any old way. 'Please, we've got to save as many of them from damage as we can.'

'We'll try,' said Mistress Paganini, but she looked uneasy. 'There are just so many . . .'

'Thank you, Mistress Paganini – I know you'll do your best,' said Duchess Catriona. The Chief Housekeeper bowed out and was immediately replaced by the Master of the Canals who said that the levels were steady but the gutters were in danger, and then Archbishop di Sarvos, who was in a state of utter panic about the churches – they were flooded, almost without exception, and some might not survive the damage.

Bianca's heart felt as if it was sinking deeper and deeper into the mucky waters with every word.

'Your Highness, news from the museum – just as we expected, it is a disaster,' said Secretary Cavassoni, face red and skirts sopping wet. 'The water is so high we were forced to drill holes in the doors before we could even get in. It's a catastrophe.'

'Are any of the paintings salvageable?' Bianca asked in a trembling voice.

'If we can stop the water soon – perhaps, a few,' said Cavassoni. 'But the damage is . . . significant. Especially to the work of Master di Lombardi.' Bianca felt her face crumble and tried to swallow back the tears. Duchess Catriona reached across the table and grabbed her hand.

'We will fix this,' she promised. 'Somehow, we will.'

Bianca wished she could believe her. She thought of all the paintings that would never be the same again, all the beautiful works of art that had been ruined forever, her grandfather's life's work . . . She had to press her sleeves against her eyes for a second, but when she looked up again her eyes were dry.

After Secretary Cavassoni had gone, there was a lull in the flood of news and reports from the city, and Duchess Catriona sagged in her chair and called for Captain Raphaeli.

'This is an act of war,' he said simply. 'I don't know how the Baron has done it, but there's no question in my mind that it's his doing.'

Bianca sat bolt upright and her jaw dropped. 'We saw him,' she whispered.

Captain Raphaeli's eyes flashed with understanding and he nodded at Bianca.

Bianca turned to the Duchess. 'We saw him do it,' she said, feeling slightly sick. 'When we were tailing him yesterday, we saw him drop something in the canal, off the Bridge of Cats. We didn't see what it was – nothing seemed to happen.'

'It's true,' said Raphaeli. 'Oscurita has struck the first blow against us. We must be prepared for the second.'

Duchess Catriona looked like she might throw something, then she nodded. 'All right. First,' she said, 'we must remove the most vulnerable citizens to buildings without any magical paintings, and we have to collect the paintings together to minimise the damage.' She sighed, and looked from Raphaeli to Franco to Bianca. 'And then . . .?'

'Their only way to attack us is through the paintings,'

said Raphaeli. 'We have to be prepared for this. Identify *all* the paintings in the city, and make sure we're ready to defend ourselves. I've already posted guards at each of the murals in the palace.'

'But that won't stop the flooding,' said Duchess Catriona. 'And it could take days. I think we need to consider dredging the canal. Perhaps we can find whatever the Baron dropped in and . . . turn it off.'

'Dredge the canal, while the whole city is draining away into it?' said Secretary Franco. 'You'll never manage it.'

Bianca stood up. 'I'm just going to get some air,' she told the Duchess. Catriona nodded, and turned her attention back to her advisors. Bianca slipped out of the room, her feet squelching on the cold, wet rug, and closed the door behind her. She started walking towards the stairs, but soon found herself half running, kicking up sprays of muddy water as she went.

She couldn't just sit in the palace and debate strategy. The Baron had done this, and then he'd vanished back to Oscurita. There had to be a painting somewhere she could get through. She would go to Oscurita, find the Baron and make him pay for destroying the art that Bianca, and her grandfather, had devoted their lives to.

The stairs were treacherously slippery and Bianca clung onto the banister as she made her way down. She passed servants carrying dripping paintings on their backs as she headed for the Duchess's rooms. She thought that she could get into the passages through the painting of the balcony. It was painted onto the wall, so they couldn't have taken it away. But when she splashed through the door she found a guard standing in front of the mural.

Where could she find a mural that hadn't been found by Raphaeli and put under guard?

Even though every door and window and drain had been opened wide to allow the water to flow out of the palace and into the canal, the entrance hall and the courtyard were knee-deep in water by the time Bianca got there. She couldn't look at the great line of paintings, leaning against each other with their bottom few feet sitting in the water and getting more and more ruined. Instead she followed the tide across the courtyard and the small, roiling river of water out of the main gates and over to the Grand Canal. Someone had managed to set up a line of sandbags across the bridge so that most of the water from the palace flowed into the canal. Bianca clambered over the sandbags onto the dry part of the bridge and stood wringing out her skirt. She could see the Bridge of Cats from here, with its black marble panthers, swarms of feral cats perching on the few dry spots. She clenched her fists. If she could swim, she would dive down herself right now, and try to find what the Baron had dropped . . .

Then she saw something. There was an unguarded mural down on the bank, on the outside wall of one of the buildings. She'd never really seen it before, or if she had she might have assumed it wasn't magical, but she was sure she could see something wet glistening on the wall and the narrow path between it and the canal.

She hurried across the bridge and down the steps to the

street to get a closer look. The mural was dim and cracked with age, and what magic it had wasn't very strong. It was a painted archway through which Bianca could glimpse beautiful flowers and trees in bloom, and a door that was supposed to look like a back entrance to the building the mural was painted on. But a thin trickle of water was seeping from under the door and wending its way across the path and into the canal.

Bianca stepped up and pulled the paintbrush key from her pocket, whispering the magic words as she did so: 'Hidden rooms, secret passages, second city.' The key folded out from the handle and she slipped it into the keyhole in the mural and turned it. As she put the brush back in her pocket she looked down at the thin stream of water again. Hopefully, this door would be further from the source of the water. She would be able to get inside, and once she was in she could find her way to Oscurita.

And then? asked a nagging voice in Bianca's mind.

And then I find the Baron and stop him, she thought. *Somehow. No matter what. There's nothing else I can do here.*

She tugged on the door, bracing herself for a small flood of water over her feet, but it seemed to be stuck – perhaps from so many years of its paint being out in all weathers. Bianca took hold of the handle in a firm grip and pulled hard, and then pulled harder.

The door burst open and a wall of water hit Bianca square in the face. She threw up her hands and squeezed her eyes shut against the onslaught, but it got into her nose and ears and she couldn't breathe or see. She staggered back towards the canal, tried to catch herself, felt her feet swept from underneath her and slipped, still blinded by the rushing water. The brick edge of the canal bank scraped against her forearms as she flailed, trying to catch onto something, anything solid. Then there was nothing but the deep, cold water of the canal.

Chapter Eleven

Bianca fought to go up, waving her arms in a tragic attempt at swimming. Her face and arms stung from the pummelling torrent and all she could see was dirty green water and churning white bubbles. Her head broke the surface for a second. She gasped in a breath of fresh canalside air and her eyes opened to take in a burst of beautiful starlight and torchlight, and then she found herself sinking again. She was too heavy, her wide skirts sodden and dragging her back down.

She held her breath, clawing at the strings that kept the material bound to her waist, but the water was so cold and her chest was burning from the lack of air. She thrashed again, peering up through strands of her own hair that waved around her head like seaweed, trying to get up to the distant and fading lights . . .

Something hit her, and she let out a bubble of surprise. Her hands closed on something long and metal, before she felt herself being dragged through the water, almost *sucked* along by the water itself, faster and faster, until the last of the light vanished and she was shooting through a small passage. She crashed against a metal grille and gasped. She was out of the water. Scraping her hair from her eyes, Bianca looked around, trying to blink away the wet and mud. She was in a tiny space, barely big enough for her to fit into lying down.

'Are you in?' It was Marco, though his voice had a strange, tinny quality.

'Wha—?' Bianca said. 'Marco?'

'Got all your limbs?'

Bianca patted herself down. Her feet and legs were there, so was her head, and her hands were shaking rather badly but definitely still attached. After a second's thought she plunged her hand into her pocket and her fingers closed around the magic paintbrush.

'Yep, I think so!'

'OK, come on up.'

Bianca twitched back as the ceiling over her head suddenly split apart and rolled back. She sat up and carefully poked her head through the hole.

'It's the underwater vehicle!' she said. She hoisted herself up and out of the hole, and found herself in a space that wasn't much bigger, but was much drier and warmer. In front of her, Marco was sitting in one of the leather seats underneath the thick glass dome, with a large wheel and an array of buttons and levers within his reach. Bits of mud and the occasional fish floated past his head. Bianca looked behind her and saw a network of pipes and bellows.

'You saved my life!' she gasped. She patted the polished copper floor of the craft. 'I'll never be sniffy about this thing again! How come you were even here?'

'Don't I have the best timing?' Marco said, throwing a grin over his shoulder at her. 'Actually, I was heading to the Bridge of Cats. I want to see if I can find out what the Baron threw in the canal in case it caused all this flooding.'

'That's a brilliant idea,' said Bianca. *A better idea than running off to Oscurita to track down the Baron by myself*, she thought. Her unexpected dip in the canal seemed to have brought her to her senses.

'Well, in theory,' said Marco. 'I haven't had any luck yet. I'm going to moor up by the palace bridge. You can get out and dry off.'

'Thanks,' Bianca said. She tried to wring out her skirt, but so much water flooded out from a single twist that she suddenly worried she might ruin the machine and actually mopped some of it up again.

The underwater craft rose to the surface and the glass dome broke through to show a dark sky above and the soft glow from the lamps in the palace. Bianca breathed a little more easily just looking at it, even though the craft bobbed worryingly as Marco steered it over to the bank, not far from where Bianca had fallen in. Luckily the canal was deserted tonight – Bianca guessed the merchants and citizens who might usually have been travelling down it were too busy trying to save their homes and paintings from the flooding.

'Hatch opening,' he said. 'Grab the rope and tie us to a mooring.'

'OK.' Bianca shifted over and picked up the coil of rope that was hanging by the hatch. There was a sucking noise and a pop, and the hatch was ajar. Bianca carefully pushed it open, stood up and barely managed to lift the weight of her dress enough to stagger out onto the canal bank. There was a rushing river of water cascading down the steps from the bridge and she was careful not to get too close, wary of the same undertow that'd dragged her off the bank last time. She knelt beside a mooring hook, carefully wrapped the rope several times around it and tied a secure knot. Then she turned around to look for the mural, wondering if the torrent was still pouring out, or if it had subsided now she'd released the pressure.

Instead of a deserted path and a river flowing into the canal from the cracked mural, she saw two guards standing by the wall. Their gold armour glowed in the light from the bridge, and the thick black paint they were using to cover the mural glistened like an oil slick.

'What are you doing?' Bianca gasped. 'That's vandalism!'

One of the guards looked around. He blinked at her in shock.

'Blimey,' he said. 'Are you all right? Did you just crawl out of the river?'

'*I'm* fine. You're the one who's going to be in trouble when the Duchess hears about this,' Bianca snapped. 'Put that brush down, right now!'

The second guard elbowed the first one. 'That's Bianca di Lombardi,' he muttered.

'Oh,' said the first guard. 'Sorry, but this is Captain's orders. And it's working, look.' He stepped back and showed her. Where the mural had been, there was a thick and clumsily painted black emptiness, like a void.

'Damn it,' muttered the second guard. 'It still needs another coat.'

Bianca leaned around them to look. A tiny trickle of water had fought its way out from underneath the black paint. Before she could stop him, the guard dipped his paintbrush in the pail of thick black paint and slapped it on, covering the hole. The water slowed and stopped.

Bianca felt sick as she watched the rest of the mural vanish under a layer of blackness. Marco had climbed out of the underwater craft, and he put his hand on her shoulder.

'Sorry, Bianca,' he muttered.

'What do you mean, Captain's orders?' Bianca growled up at the guards.

'I mean, Captain Raphaeli told us to grab a pail and a brush and paint over any murals we saw that were leaking,' said the guard.

'Really,' Bianca said flatly. 'Raphaeli told you to do this?' She clenched her fists and turned around, almost walking into Marco. She shoved past him and started up the steps to the bridge two at a time. When she got to the top, she ran across the bridge, clambered over the sandbags and splashed down in the water, fighting her way to the gates against the current. It was hard going with the water still pouring around her feet and her dress weighing her down as surely as if she'd tied a bunch of rocks to her shoulders.

The palace's paintings were still stacked in the middle of the courtyard, leaking water from their painted doors and windows. But there seemed to be a little less water in the courtyard. Bianca knew she should've been happy to see it, but it just made her heart sink. She crossed the yard to the palace doors, and looked inside. There were two more guards, each with a brush and a pail of thick black paint, destroying murals on either side of the great hall. On her left, the rolling hillsides of the Vine Country vanished under a layer of paint, and on her right, thick black drips streaked down the face of an angel so that it seemed to weep black tears. As the paint covered it and the church door it stood in front of, the beating of its wings slowed, faltered and then stopped altogether.

Bianca wiped hot tears from her cold cheeks with one wet, grubby sleeve.

How could they do this? How could they bring themselves to destroy the city's legacy like this? Didn't they care that they were painting over years of some artist's devotion?

Three servants carried paintings past her, walking carefully so as not to slip on the mud that caked the floors. Bianca turned to watch them, and the servants didn't even bother keeping the paintings upright! They threw them onto the pile any old way and hurried back inside.

Bianca was about to shout at them for being so careless, when she saw Duchess Catriona and Captain Raphaeli standing together on a flight of steps at the side of the courtyard, out of the water. Duchess Catriona was looking at the paintings and her face was paler than Bianca had ever seen it. She looked as if she might throw up. Instead she gave a single nod.

What are they . . .?

A guard with a flaming torch appeared.

No! They wouldn't. They couldn't . . .

Bianca wanted to run and tackle him and stop this, but it seemed as if it all happened in an instant – she breathed in, she saw another guard with a large bucket throw its oily contents onto the paintings, she smelled pitch and saw the fiery torch lowered to the canvas.

'No!' Bianca yelled, but it was too late. The palace's paintings, the treasure of La Luminosa, caught alight. 'No!' she screamed again, her voice cracking as the flames licked around the landscapes, portraits, scenes from the city's history and legends, saints and knights, masterpieces and minor works. She splashed across the courtyard to the bottom of the steps where the Duchess and Captain stood, and glared up at them. She was still dripping with canal water and starting to tremble from the cold and the boiling anger that flooded her veins, but she clenched her fists and stomped up the stairs, as close as she dared.

'How could you?' she gasped. 'You can't do this!'

Captain Raphaeli stared down at her with a mix of sympathy and horror in his face.

'Bianca, you're wet through,' he said. 'Did you try to get through the passages?'

'I . . . Yes, I did,' she said.

'What were you going to do, against the whole city of Oscurita?' Raphaeli scolded her. 'How could you think of attempting that?'

Bianca shook her head, resentful of him trying to distract her from her fury. 'How could you do *this*?' She glanced back at the flames licking around the frames of the paintings, then turned to Duchess Catriona. 'These paintings are the heart and soul of La Luminosa! They're irreplaceable! What's the point in defeating Edita if we're going to sacrifice everything we care about to do it? What will be left to defend in La Luminosa if we destroy its heart like this?'

'It wasn't an easy decision,' Catriona half whispered. She looked as still and pale as a statue, with the firelight flickering on her face.

'And what about my mother? If we cut her off completely she might not be able to take back the throne!'

'It's dreadful,' said Captain Raphaeli, firmly but with a gentleness that surprised Bianca. 'But we have a duty – to protect our Duchess, to protect *all* the citizens of La Luminosa. If the Oscuritans invade and take over the city, having the paintings won't be much of a consolation.'

'We knew Edita could use the passages to invade before this!' Bianca snapped.

'And we all should have listened to you,' said Raphaeli. 'But we didn't. We're making up for it now. I won't allow La Luminosa to come to harm, even if it means burning every painting in the city.'

'But I didn't want this!' Bianca looked round at the bonfire of masterpieces. She could feel herself begin to weep.

'Bianca, look,' said Marco's voice. He was standing at the bottom of the steps, pointing towards the palace gate. A terrible parade of guards was coming across the bridge, carrying dripping paintings under their arms. Bianca even recognised some of the pictures – she'd helped di Lombardi paint them.

'Please,' she begged, looking up at Captain Raphaeli. 'Don't do this.'

'I don't have a choice,' Raphaeli said.

'Stop! Please stop!' cried a woman's voice. Bianca looked around to see a plump, middle-aged woman dressed in a green cloak over a fine cotton nightdress, running alongside one of the guards. 'You have to listen to me! You cannot burn that painting!'

Bianca and Marco glanced at each other and Bianca ran down the steps into the water – which was much lower now, and mostly mud – and squelched past the bonfire of paintings towards the woman.

'Can't you see it?' the woman cried, gesturing to the portrait of a young girl that one of the guards was carrying. 'It isn't leaking. It isn't even magical!'

'Like I told you the last eighty times, Captain's orders are to burn the paintings,' the guard growled at her.

'Please.' The woman ran her hands through her fine grey hair in despair. 'Please, that painting's been in my family for a hundred years, since before magical paints even existed in La Luminosa!'

'Stop!' Bianca shouted, sliding the last few feet across the muddy stones to the woman's side. 'She's right, it's not leaking.'

The guard gave Bianca a filthy look. 'And just why should I listen to some drowned rat of a girl?' he asked.

Bianca drew herself up as tall as she could and tried to give him her best Duchess Catriona impression – which was a little bit harder than normal as her hair was still plastered to her head with dirty canal water and her dress was splattered with mud.

'Because I am Bianca di Lombardi, Master di Lombardi's granddaughter, and his apprentice. I know what I'm talking about!' she said. The guard gave her a sceptical look. She peered around the man's arm at the painting. It definitely wasn't leaking – and the little girl in the picture showed no sign of breath or movement. She was sitting in a sun-dappled garden underneath a tall oak tree. There wasn't even any illusion of space between her and the background – the painting was completely flat and still. 'I'm telling you, that painting is no threat to the city!'

The guard hesitated for just a second, and then shrugged. 'Makes no difference to me,' he said. 'I was told to burn the paintings, and that's what I'm doing.'

'Why won't you *listen*?' The woman in the green cloak reached over and tried to snatch the painting out of his hands. The guard gripped it harder and gave the woman a shove that made her lose her footing in the mud and fall over. She landed on her back in the water.

Marco rushed to help her up, but Bianca braced herself to leap on the guard as he splashed a few steps closer to the burning pile of paintings.

'Stop there,' said Captain Raphaeli. This time, the guard stopped. He looked up at the Captain approaching him across the courtyard and tried to snap a salute without letting go of the painting.

'Sir!' he said.

'Let me see that, Corporal.'

111

'Sir, yes, sir.' The guard handed the painting to Raphaeli, who held it up and examined it in the light from the fire. He ran his hand around each edge and then turned back to the woman, who was standing, dripping mud and leaning gratefully on Marco's arm.

'Please accept my deepest apologies, Mistress . . .?'

'Mistress Frazetti,' said the woman.

'Mistress Frazetti,' said Raphaeli. 'I am so sorry. There has obviously been a mistake – this painting is not magical.' He handed it back to the woman, who clutched it with tears shining in her eyes. 'You may keep it.'

'Oh, thank you!' she said. She hurried away, as if wanting to get the painting home before the Captain changed his mind. Raphaeli turned to the guard with a glower.

'As for you – we will have a talk about pushing old ladies around when all this is over. For the moment, I want you positioned at the end of the bridge, all night, checking each painting to make sure it's actually magical. If it's not leaking out water, and it doesn't have a magical door in it, it doesn't need to be burned. Don't let me hear any complaints that you've let any slip through.'

'Yes, sir,' the guard mumbled.

'What are you waiting for? Go!' Captain Raphaeli pointed, and the guard scurried off, stopping every other guard he passed to check their paintings for magical doorways.

'Thank you, Captain,' said Bianca. She watched as one of the guards was checked, his painting was found to be leaking, and he walked up to throw it on the fire. 'But, please – is there really no way we can save the magical paintings, too?'

112

'What else can we do?' Captain Raphaeli sighed. 'I cannot leave the paintings lying around the city, waiting for the Baron to march through with an army and catch us unawares.'

'Put a guard on them,' Bianca said, without really believing it was an option – there were just too many, all over the city. Captain Raphaeli opened his mouth, probably to say just that, but then a bright spark of an idea hit Bianca. 'Put a guard on them!' she repeated. 'Gather all the paintings together and put them in the Museum of Art. We can lock the doors and guard the building, while we find a way to stop Oscurita from invading.'

'That could take a long time,' Captain Raphaeli pointed out. 'And what's more, we can't possibly save every painting. The museum doesn't have enough space, unless we pile them high – and with them leaking like this, that would damage them so badly we might as well have burned them.'

'Then send for the artists in residence,' said Bianca, her face lighting up despite the pain in her heart. 'Get them to identify the most valuable, the most important paintings, and send those to the museum, and . . . and . . .'

'And burn the rest,' said Marco quietly. 'It could work!' Bianca gave him a grateful look, for finishing the sentence she couldn't bring herself to say.

'We would save *something*,' she said.

'All right, all right,' Raphaeli said. He stepped in front of the next guard who was approaching the fire, and held up his arm. 'Take this back to the bridge and don't bring any more paintings into the palace. Tell the others to keep rounding up pictures from the city – Master Cosimo and

Mistress Lucia will be examining the paintings and sending some to the museum. We'll build another fire in the museum courtyard so we can get this mud cleared out of the palace. You!' he shouted across the courtyard to the guard who'd pushed Mistress Frazetti down. 'Run to the master artists' suite and rouse them.' The guard looked panicked for a moment, and then ran across the courtyard, slipping and sliding, towards the palace entrance.

'Thank you,' Bianca said softly, watching the line of guards with paintings slowly begin to turn around and head back out of the palace gates. She looked up at Captain Raphaeli and then glanced behind him to Duchess Catriona, who was sitting on the flight of steps now, without much of a care for the state of her gown. She caught Bianca's eye and patted her heart twice, and mouthed *well done*.

'We still have to paint over the murals and frescos that can't be moved,' said the Captain. 'But we'll save as many as we can. Now, if you'll excuse me, I have much more work to do.'

Bianca was starting to feel the strain of spending her night running, shouting and falling in the water as she and Marco walked to the palace gate to watch a line of guards and volunteers carrying paintings come to a halt. The city's church bells rang out for one in the morning as they backed up along the bridge. Water still poured from most of the paintings, and soon both sides of the bridge looked like an endlessly cascading waterfall. A few minutes later, Cosimo and Lucia splashed through the mud, yawning. Bianca stifled a sympathy yawn as she watched them hurry up to the front of the line of paintings and instruct the first guard to hold his up.

They were fully dressed, and Bianca remembered that they had been the very first to notice the paintings beginning to leak – the artists' suite in the palace was probably mostly underwater soon after, so they couldn't have had any sleep. Although at least, she thought, shivering against her sticky wet dress, they hadn't rushed off to be heroes and fallen into the canal.

She groaned as she saw Cosimo shake his head at the first guard, who shouldered his painting again and headed back across the bridge. 'I wish I could be the one to choose what we could save.'

'You should be glad you don't have to make those decisions,' Marco told her gently.

Bianca watched as Cosimo and Lucia debated the value of a rough, but definitely magical di Lombardi sketch of the palace versus a large landscape that showed a lapping seashore. Despite the watery theme, the only door in the painting was on a small boat in the distance – water dribbled from it, but only a few drops at a time.

'Which of those is worth more?' Marco asked her. 'Which will be most valuable to their grandchildren in a hundred years' time? Could you really choose, knowing the other one will be destroyed?'

Cosimo tapped the palace sketch and Bianca's heart instantly ached for the seashore painting.

'You're right. I couldn't. All these paintings are precious to me. Every one. Even Filpepi's.'

Marco linked his arm through hers and gave it a squeeze. 'Ew, you're still soggy!' he said, but he didn't let go.

Bianca smiled gratefully at him, and turned away from the terrible sight of the art of La Luminosa being studied, judged, and then sent away. A few lucky paintings would be hidden in the museum, tainted by the damp, but still existing. The rest . . .

She stared hard into the flames that still burned in the middle of the courtyard.

The rest would be consumed by flames.

Chapter Twelve

'So, you tried to get to Oscurita?' said the Duchess's voice behind them. Bianca turned to see Catriona walking across the courtyard, her fine skirts swishing through the mud. The burning pile of paintings was still aflame, hot and bright, but it must have destroyed the magic in most of them because there was only a thin cloud of steam trickling from the pile now, and even less coming from inside the palace.

'I didn't even get through the door,' Bianca admitted. 'I tried to get in through a mural down by the canal, and I got washed right off the path and into the water. I would've drowned if Marco hadn't come along in Master di Lombardi's underwater craft.'

'A craft? That goes underwater?' Duchess Catriona's face lit up, and some colour returned to it for the first time since the paintings had started leaking. 'That sounds fantastic!' She looked at Marco. 'But what on earth were you doing in the canal in the middle of the night?'

'Trying to find out what the Baron da Russo dropped into the canal,' said Marco. 'It was the only suspicious thing we saw him do all day. I'm *sure* it must have something to do with the flooding. I couldn't find anything, though – and then Bianca fell in.'

'Where's this craft now?' said Duchess Catriona.

'We moored it up on the other side of the bridge,' said Bianca.

'Oh really?' The Duchess's eyes sparkled, and she hitched up her skirts and strode out of the palace gate.

'Duchess, wait!' Marco said, and he and Bianca exchanged slightly stunned looks before following her.

Duchess Catriona bustled past Cosimo and Lucia with a 'Masters, thank you for this – carry on', and hopped over the sandbags. With the paintings in the palace burned and the city paintings lined up on the bridge, there was now more water on the far side of the bags, but the Duchess didn't even blink as she plunged her feet into the cold water. The guards holding their paintings hurriedly tried to bow to her. Bianca and Marco followed in the Duchess's wake as she swept across the bridge.

'Duchess! What are you doing?' Captain Raphaeli ran up behind them. 'You must not leave the palace until we have the paintings secured!'

'I'm going to fix the leak,' Duchess Catriona called over her shoulder.

'What are you up to now?' Raphaeli demanded of Bianca, as all four of them reached the steps down to the canal bank.

She's going for a ride in the underwater machine, Bianca thought, with a small smile, but didn't say anything to Raphaeli.

Duchess Catriona gasped with pleasure and clapped her

hands together at the sight of the underwater craft bobbing in the water, its glass and wood and brass surface still gleaming despite a coating of canal water.

'How wonderful,' she said, and started down the steps. 'Master di Lombardi was so clever!'

'No, Your Highness!' Captain Raphaeli said, following her down. 'I cannot allow you to get in that thing.'

'*Allow* me?' Duchess Catriona said, turning so sharply Raphaeli almost ran into her. 'I think you'll find I am still the ruler of this city. *I* shall allow *you* to accompany us if you must, but we're going to fix this, tonight.'

'There really isn't room for four,' Marco said. 'There's barely room for three.'

'You can take my place, Captain,' Bianca volunteered hopefully.

'No, he can't,' Marco said. 'We might need you if something goes wrong.'

Bianca deflated a little, but she didn't argue.

'I won't let the three of you go off in this thing,' Raphaeli said. 'Absolutely not.'

'Captain Raphaeli, I am an adult, and I am Duchess, and I can take care of myself. This is a direct order. *Direct order*, Raphaeli.'

'I . . . I . . .' Captain Raphaeli ground his teeth. 'Yes, Your Highness. But *please* be careful, all of you.'

'It's perfectly safe,' Marco said, opening the craft's hatch and sliding into the main driver's seat. 'See?'

Raphaeli shook his head. 'If you're not back in ten minutes, I'm coming in after you.' He peeled off his cloak, breastplate, greaves and heavy gloves and started to roll up his shirt sleeves.

'You do that,' said Catriona, stepping into the craft and settling in the cargo section behind the seats.

Bianca gave the Captain an apologetic smile, then untied the rope from the mooring hook and very carefully eased herself into the second leather seat. Marco closed the hatch and started the bellows pumping. The craft sank slowly under the water.

Bianca turned to look at Duchess Catriona. Despite the nasty sinking feeling and the sight of the canal closing over their heads, she couldn't help smiling. That was much more like the Duchess she remembered!

'Good thing Secretary Franco wasn't with us just then,' Bianca said. 'He would have had an absolute fit!'

'Oh, who cares what Franco thinks,' said Catriona, staring up in wonder at the dark water through the glass dome. 'He's got a fantastic political brain, you know, but there isn't a grain of adventure in him.' She grinned at Bianca. 'I can't always let you two have all the fun, can I?'

The water in the canal was getting darker and muddier. Marco steered them around in a semicircle, with his eyes firmly set on the dials and instruments in front of him, until they were heading back towards the Bridge of Cats.

'What's *that*?' Duchess Catriona said. Bianca looked just in time to see something with more than four legs scuttle across the glass dome and leap off into the water.

'I have no idea,' Bianca said. 'I didn't know anything like that lived in the canals . . .'

Marco flicked a couple of switches and the water just ahead of them lit up. 'It's got an oil lamp in its nose,' Marco said. 'This ought to help.'

Despite her misgivings, Bianca couldn't help but stare in wonder as the light shone through the swirling water. Something huge and stony loomed up in front of them and Marco had to scramble to turn them so they wouldn't run into it. As they passed, Bianca saw an enormous nose and deep black eyes in a face that lay sideways in the mud.

'It's a statue of the old god of the sea,' said Catriona, her voice soft with wonder. 'It used to be on the bank just here but it fell into the canal in a storm.'

Marco corrected their course and they chugged onwards towards the bridge.

'This craft is so amazing,' the Duchess said. 'What does this do?' Bianca heard a hiss and splash, and twisted in her seat, her heart in her mouth. 'Oops!' Duchess Catriona hurriedly screwed a cap back onto a copper pipe, her face and hands dripping with water. 'Sorry,' she said, when Bianca and Marco both stared at her. 'I'll leave the engineering to you two.'

A minute or two later, Marco squinted at a dial in front of him. 'I think we're by the Bridge of Cats now,' he said. 'I'm going to take us all the way down to the bottom so we can see what's on the canal bed.'

Bianca's ears felt slightly odd as they dropped the last few feet to the very bottom of the canal.

'Bianca, grab that handle and wind it a couple of times,' Marco said, pointing to a handle just beside Bianca's head.

121

She took hold of it and gave it a couple of turns, until she saw something glinting in the water in front of them. It was like a metal hand on the end of a long metal arm.

'That's the thing you grabbed me with,' Bianca said.

'If you can pick something up with it, then we can suck it into the chamber,' said Marco. 'The controls are in front of you.'

Bianca laid her hands on two levers. When she twitched the left one, the arm moved from left to right in front of her, and when she moved the right one the arm went up and down. She investigated the other buttons around the two levers and found that there was one with a neat label bolted just underneath it that said 'GRASP'. She pushed it, and the finger parts curled in towards the flat metal palm.

'Right!' she said. 'Let's see what's down here.'

Manoeuvring the hand was extremely tricky at first – the controls were sensitive, and it seemed to Bianca that all she had to do was breathe on them for them to send the arm sweeping through the water, dropping whatever lumpy or shiny thing she'd been trying to pick up. But after a few tries, she got the hang of it and had even managed to learn when to hit the grasp button to hold her catch still so that the others could see it.

She held up several ordinary shells and one enormous one the size of her head, enough copper coins to pay for an apple cake from the stall on the Piazza del Fiero, and a strange ball that bounced and floated whenever she moved the metal arm. They stared at it for several minutes, wondering if it was magic, before it turned over and Bianca spotted the faint, faded remains of a clumsily painted string of daisies on the side.

'It's just a child's ball,' she said.

'I didn't realise there was so much rubbish under the bridges,' Duchess Catriona muttered. 'As soon as things get back to normal, I'm definitely going to have the canals cleaned.'

'Wait, what's that?' Marco pointed at an odd, lumpy shape half buried under the silt.

Bianca narrowed her eyes and pushed the arm forward, hooking two of the metal fingers around the thing. She lifted it up.

'It's a shoe,' she said, and dropped it again.

'Oh,' said Marco.

'We can't give up,' said the Duchess, an edge of sadness creeping into her voice. 'We've got to fix this!'

'Well, we'll have to resurface soon to let in some fresh air anyway,' said Marco.

Bianca stared down at the canal bed. She opened her mouth to agree – perhaps it would be better to wait until morning, or . . .

'Wait,' she whispered.

'The other shoe?' Duchess Catriona asked.

Bianca didn't answer, irrationally afraid to breathe too hard in case it disturbed the silt at the bottom of the canal. There was something there, something odd. She knew she'd seen it. Now she just needed to see it again.

'There!' She pointed. 'Did you see that? Some of that pile of mud just . . . vanished!' She grabbed the arm's controls and slid its fingers into the mud and then up and out with a smooth motion. The particles of mud poured off the hand, leaving behind something round and dull, about the size of a large orange, flattened out.

Marco and the Duchess leaned forward as Bianca punched the grasp button and then pumped the suction lever as hard as she could. The round object was dragged out of the hand and Catriona jumped as they heard it rattle into the compartment underneath her.

'Closing the suction pipe,' said Marco. There was a clang and a gurgling noise, and then a pop. Marco twisted in his chair. 'You can open the hatch now. Let's see what we've got.'

Duchess Catriona tugged open the trapdoor and reached down into the little space Bianca had climbed out of. She pulled the disc out and wiped the mud off it on the edge of her dress.

'It's . . . odd,' she said. 'It's an engraving.'

Bianca took it from the Duchess and peered at it. The engraving was a picture of an open door in a brick wall covered in intricate trailing ivy, with a stone passage visible on the other side. She held it in her hands, listening to the way it seemed to speak to her – not with sound, but with a tingling, pulling feeling that she'd only felt a few times before.

'This is from Oscurita,' she said. 'I'm sure of it. I can feel it.' She touched the open door, half expecting her fingers to go right through. If the water was pouring into the passages through this magic engraving, she should've been able to reach inside the passages through the same opening. But they stopped at the surface.

'Let's get it back to the palace.'

'Going up,' said Marco, and he released a catch, pumped the bellows, and the underwater craft started to rise to the surface.

Bianca frowned at the disc in her hands as the water bubbled and churned around them. 'It's magic, definitely – but what kind?'

Secretary Franco leaned over the table, peering down at the disc. It had a hole right through it, just above the carving of the door, as if it was meant to be worn as a medallion.

'But the water is still coming,' said Captain Raphaeli.

Secretary Franco, Captain Raphaeli and an impressively large number of guards had met them when they'd moored the craft by the Bridge of Cats and marched them swiftly back inside the palace. Now they were in the Duchess's rooms, and Secretary Franco was casting sceptical glances between the medallion and the mural in the room, which hadn't been painted over yet and was still spilling water forth at the same steady rate as before. A servant with a mop was standing by it, emptying the water into a series of buckets that another servant took away to empty every few minutes. It was a literally endless job, and Bianca was incredibly grateful it wasn't hers.

Duchess Catriona was sitting on her couch beside the low table, Marco beside her, staring at the medallion with a seething dislike. But that hadn't stopped the flooding either.

'That just means it's not directly connected to the passages,' Bianca said. 'But I'm sure it's magic, and we saw the Baron drop it in the water just before the flood started.'

'What about your magic key?' Marco asked.

Bianca shrugged, took out the paintbrush and whispered the magic words. She saw Secretary Franco stare, wide-eyed, as the key unfolded from the paintbrush handle, but then he looked away and tried to pretend not to be interested. Several of the guards stared openly as she held up the medallion and tried to find a way to fit the key into it.

'The door's too small to shut, and anyway it doesn't move,' she said. 'It's an engraving, not a painting, so I don't think I could get it to move with an *animare*.'

'All right, what about the normal paint?' Marco suggested. 'The non-magic stuff that the Captain's been using on the murals?'

Captain Raphaeli ordered a guard to fetch the paint, and Bianca made a face as it was placed on the table beside the medallion. She didn't want to touch the stuff, knowing what damage it had done – but this was too important for her to let her resentments stop her. She dipped Master di Lombardi's brush in the thick, black paint – sending up an apology for the insult – and painted over the top of the engraving.

Everybody turned and watched the water trickling from the mural. The servant kept mopping, his eyes fixed on the gap under the door to the balcony. The water didn't stop. In fact, to the servant's obvious dismay, it seemed to flow a little bit faster.

Bianca looked down at the medallion, and found that the black paint had run off the disc and onto the table. Not a drop of it had managed to stick, even though when she touched the engraving it was perfectly dry.

'What do we do now?' she asked.

'We must remove the disc to a safe place and keep studying it carefully,' said Secretary Franco. '*Much* was risked to bring it out of the canal,' he added, shooting a disapproving glare at Duchess Catriona. He had already made his feelings about the Duchess's trip in the underwater craft very clear, but Bianca could tell he wasn't planning to stop rebuking her for it any time soon. 'It's obviously of foreign make, even if it isn't actually the cause of the flooding. It may not be doing anything at all.'

Duchess Catriona suddenly leapt to her feet in a rustle of damp red silk.

'Well, there's one way to find out for certain,' she said. She walked over to the fireplace and grabbed the iron poker from its holder beside the grate.

'Your Highness, stop!' Secretary Franco called out, but it was too late – Duchess Catriona strode back to the small table, raised the poker and brought it down point-first in the centre of the medallion. The disc cracked and there was a noise like breaking glass. Duchess Catriona brought the poker down on the disc again and again, until it lay in pieces in a pile of its own dust.

Bianca stared at her, impressed and fascinated and trying to suppress a grin, until finally the Duchess lowered the poker and stepped back, breathing heavily.

'It's stopped!' said a voice. Everyone turned to look at the servant, who was standing, leaning on his mop with a broad grin on his face. There was no more water trickling from the painted door. He swept up the last of the water and no more pooled at the base of the wall. 'Bless you, Milady, you stopped the flood!'

Duchess Catriona dropped the poker onto the table with a clang and gave Secretary Franco a polite and slightly exhausted smile. 'My Lord, I respect your counsel greatly,' she said. 'But sometimes a Duchess just has to *do something*.'

Bianca caught Marco's eye, and then looked away again quickly, in serious danger of collapsing with helpless laughter.

Chapter Thirteen

A few seconds later, Bianca heard a voice in the corridor let out a shout of happiness. The servant with the mop ran out and she heard him shout, 'It was the Duchess! She stopped the flooding!'

Bianca grinned and bobbed a damp curtsey to Duchess Catriona, then ran to the window. She could just about see over the walls to the bridge, and though she couldn't see the paintings clearly, there was a definite ripple of astonishment through the people on the bridge as they noticed that the flood had stopped. An excited chatter went up from the guards, and then they joined in the cheer, 'God bless the Duchess. God save La Luminosa!'

It seemed to echo across the whole city. Bianca was certain she could hear a roar of happiness from the streets across the canal. Had the whole city been awake and bailing out their homes and squares? A second later, bells started to ring from the Church of San Fernando, and other churches and chapels joined in. The night was alive with starlight and jangling bells, and Bianca turned back to the room with a huge grin on her face.

'God bless the Duchess,' she said.

With a quick glance between them, the guards all dropped to one knee. Captain Raphaeli and Marco joined them, and so did Secretary Franco, with a creak of his old joints and a small grunt.

Duchess Catriona looked extremely pleased, but waved them all up quickly. 'I wish this was the end of our troubles,' she said. 'But we still have a missing delegation from Oscurita who could return through the secret passages at any moment.'

'Quite right, Your Highness,' said Captain Raphaeli. 'Our next move should be to finish painting over all of the magical murals and rounding up the paintings to be locked up or destroyed. The frescos will be easier to deal with now that they're not leaking water to wash away our paint.'

'Wait.' Bianca frowned. 'You can't think of still burning the paintings now that the flood has stopped?'

'Even without the flood, what I said before still holds true,' said Captain Raphaeli. 'I will not take risks with the security of La Luminosa.'

'Of course, we'll have to shut down the studios as well,' pointed out Secretary Franco. He turned to Bianca. 'Lady Bianca, can we trust you to make sure that the ingredients to make more magical paintings are kept safe under lock and key?'

'I . . . Yes, I suppose so,' Bianca stammered. She felt shocked and stupid all at once – she'd thought that stopping the leak would save the paintings, and she didn't know why she'd let herself believe it.

'Good,' said Captain Raphaeli. 'We're all tired, but we must secure the city. Before noon, I want there to be no way for anyone to access the secret passages, from anywhere.'

No way to get to the secret passages. No way to get to the studio, or Oscurita. No way to see my mother. I never got to say goodbye . . .

'But what about my mother?' Bianca cried. 'She's still in Oscurita, trying to rally the Resistance against Edita – we should be supporting her, not cutting her off!' She turned to Duchess Catriona. 'Please, Duchess, don't let them destroy any more paintings. I'm sure we can find a . . .'

Duchess Catriona shook her head. 'I'm sorry, Bianca, this is the only –' she broke off to stifle a huge yawn.

'Your Highness, you must get some rest,' said Secretary Franco. 'Is your bedchamber still dry?'

'Relatively,' said Duchess Catriona.

'Then I suggest you get some sleep – our plan will take several hours to complete, and we will need you to be on your best form later.'

Duchess Catriona nodded, and with a last sympathetic-but-firm smile at Bianca, she left the room.

Marco walked over to Bianca and gave her shoulder a squeeze. 'It's OK,' he said. 'We've stopped the damage to the paintings, and Captain Raphaeli is going to save as many as he can. It's not the end of the world.'

'I know,' Bianca sighed. 'It's just those paintings were Master di Lombardi's legacy. They were his *life*.'

'Well, it's worth it if we can avoid a real war, isn't it? That's his legacy, too. He wanted there to be peace between La Luminosa and Oscurita.'

Bianca had to admit he had a point . . .

'Plus,' said Marco with a suddenly bright smile, 'just think of how many walls in the palace are going to need repainting after this is over! Every artist in the city is going to be busy for the rest of their lives replacing everything that's been lost.'

'That's true,' Bianca said, the beginnings of a smile crossing her face. It was a beautiful thought, like a tiny glimmer of light at the bottom of a deep, dark well. She couldn't help imagining the great art that Lucia and Cosimo, the other artists' studios and she herself, would create in the places where the murals had been . . .

'With one restriction,' said Secretary Franco. 'There are to be no more magical paintings. Not ever. I won't risk this happening again.'

'No. No!' Bianca gasped. 'You can't outlaw magical paints! That's barbaric!'

'It's necessary,' said Franco. 'Even if we win the war with Oscurita and put Saralinda on the throne – which I have to tell you is doubtful – how can we know some rogue agent won't do exactly the same as the Baron did, or worse? The only way to make sure we're safe is to destroy the passages, forever, and that means no more magical paints.'

'No . . .' Bianca shook her head. 'That's like saying we can't build boats because someone might come over the sea and attack us! That's crazy! What's more, the Duchess would never, ever agree to that – and I'm going to show you that right now.'

She stomped across the room and tugged on the door, but, to her surprise, it was locked. She knocked, hard.

'Duchess Catriona, I'm sorry to disturb you,' she said through the door. 'It's important.'

'Don't you dare disturb the Duchess's sleep!' Secretary Franco snapped.

'She won't be asleep yet – and she won't mind, either,' Bianca said. She knocked again. 'Please, Duchess, it'll only take a second. Secretary Franco has his head stuffed up . . . somewhere really stupid,' she finished, after a warning look from Captain Raphaeli.

There was no answer from inside the bedchamber.

She can't have fallen asleep that fast, Bianca thought. *Can she?*

'Duchess?' she said again. 'I'm sorry to wake you, really . . .'

Still no reply.

There was a long, weightless pause in the room.

'Duchess Catriona?' Captain Raphaeli gently moved Bianca aside and spoke through the door. 'I can have Lady Bianca removed from your chambers if you wish.'

Bianca put her hands on her hips in annoyance, but then Raphaeli glanced back at her and she saw that his brows were drawn down with worry.

'*Damn* it,' Raphaeli muttered under his breath. 'I apologise for this, Your Highness!' He stood back, raised one foot and kicked at the bedchamber door. He didn't waste time drawing back, but kicked hard on the same spot four times until the wood split around the handle and the door burst open. Raphaeli ran inside, his hand on his sword hilt. Bianca followed him in, with Marco and Secretary Franco close on her heels.

There was nobody in the room. Bianca stared around at it in confusion and a growing, creeping horror.

The only door to this room was the one she'd just walked through. The Duchess couldn't have left the room without walking past everyone who was standing in her drawing room. Raphaeli went to the window and looked out, but Bianca knew it was a long drop, straight down.

Bianca walked slowly to the bed, desperately hoping this was one of Catriona's less amusing pranks and she would sit up from under the covers . . . but when Bianca pulled them back there was nothing. No Catriona, and nowhere for anyone to hide.

Bianca heard Secretary Franco and Captain Raphaeli leaping into action, giving orders to the guards. She ignored them. Everything seemed to slow down, and every tiny sensation seemed huge and overwhelming.

There *was* something in the bed – a round disc. For a second, Bianca thought that it might be the one that had caused the flooding, but it was different – it wasn't smashed, and instead of an engraving of an open door it was white marble, and completely plain. She gingerly picked it up and held it for the others to see.

'More Oscuritan magic?' Secretary Franco growled. 'What does it do? What has it done to the Duchess?'

Bianca shook her head miserably as she handed it over to him, unable to answer.

She backed away, and felt crunching under her feet. At first she thought it was just yet more mud, but then she looked down. The floor was almost dry, and the only mud was from the footprints that she, Marco and the guards had made when they came in. The painting that'd hung on the wall had been removed and the floor cleaned almost immediately after the flood began.

So what was the white, crunchy substance Bianca found when she stepped back? She bent down and picked up a pinch of the stuff and turned some of it between her thumb and forefinger. The white shards had quite sharp, jagged edges.

'Sound the alarm,' Captain Raphaeli was saying, and when Bianca looked up at him he looked as if he'd seen a ghost. 'Duchess Catriona has been taken.'

135

Chapter Fourteen

'Wait!' Secretary Franco raised a wrinkled hand. 'Don't sound the alarm. News of the Duchess's disappearance should not leave this room, not yet.'

What? Bianca dropped the white substance and turned to stare at Franco. 'Have you gone completely mental?' she asked. 'We have to find her!'

Captain Raphaeli's hand tightened on the hilt of his sword and he stepped close to Franco. Bianca suddenly remembered Raphaeli's reputation – he was a reasonable man, but not one you wanted to get on the wrong side of.

'I will not leave the Duchess in danger,' he growled. 'She will not be used for some . . . some political bargaining chip! I should not have let her out of my sight, not for an instant.'

'Unless you planned to sleep at the foot of her bed like a dog, you couldn't have stopped this,' said Secretary Franco.

'I should have stopped it. It was my *job* to stop it!' Raphaeli slammed his fist down on the Duchess's dresser beside him. The whole room seemed to rattle, and Bianca and Marco both jumped. To his credit, Secretary Franco barely blinked. 'I should have trusted my instincts and cut off the Baron's head where he stood when he first came through the painting – instead I let him slip through my fingers, *again*.'

Bianca remembered watching as the Baron da Russo and Piero Filpepi had vanished through the magical trapdoor to Oscurita. Captain Raphaeli hadn't been able to reach them in time.

'I have no intention of leaving the Duchess in danger, Captain,' said Secretary Franco, quietly. 'I believe our best chance of bringing her back quickly and unharmed is to do it in secret. An invasion is clearly imminent, and it won't help our chances if the people panic. Let them focus on Duchess Catriona's role in stopping the flood. Meanwhile . . .' He hesitated, drawing a deep breath, as if he was going to have to say something he didn't like. Then he turned and looked directly at Bianca.

'Bianca, I want you to be completely honest with me now. Is it true that your mother is the true Duchess of Oscurita, and that she has assembled a number of Resistance fighters?'

'Yes,' she said.

'And is it true that you yourself can see and move around in Oscurita?'

'Yes!' Bianca said, angry that he doubted her word . . . and then she realised what he was planning. 'Yes, I can.'

'No, Franco. No.' Captain Raphaeli shook his head, clearly realising the plan too. 'We can't send her in alone – she's a child!'

'I'm the only person who can do it, though,' Bianca said. 'Marco's an acrobat, and even he was always falling over things when he came to Oscurita with me.'

'Thanks,' Marco muttered.

'The Resistance will help me,' Bianca added. 'And I know how to find them.'

'I don't propose sending Bianca in to fight the war by herself,' Franco explained to Captain Raphaeli. 'But it seems clear to me that Duchess Catriona has been spirited away with Oscuritan magic. She may be in Oscurita, or hidden in some secret place between the cities like Bianca's painted passages.'

'Smashing the medallion worked last time,' Marco pointed out. 'Do you think if we break this one . . .'

They all stared at the perfectly white disc in Secretary Franco's hand.

'I wouldn't,' said Captain Raphaeli. 'If we do she may be trapped wherever she is, maybe forever. We can't risk it.'

'Either way, we know the Oscuritans are behind this. We need someone to go there and find out what they've done with the Duchess and how we can get her back.' Franco looked at Bianca. 'Nobody else but her can move around Oscurita without drawing attention to themselves.'

Raphaeli shook his head. 'Sending children after children,' he muttered. But he finally let his hand slip from the hilt of his sword. 'How shall we get her through? If we're keeping the Duchess's kidnapping a secret, I wouldn't advise marching Bianca down to the museum to slip in through one of the paintings there. The place will still be swarming with people – and if I was an Oscuritan spy, that's where I'd want to be.'

'Can you paint yourself a door?' Marco asked. 'She's done it before, you know,' he added proudly. 'She painted us out of a prison tower.'

Bianca smiled at him. 'I might be able to – if I have the materials. There should be some in the artist-in-residence suite.'

'Then let's go,' Secretary Franco said. 'And remember, not a word to anyone about the Duchess.'

The artist in residence's tiny studio had not had its floors cleaned – they were starting to dry out, but they were still caked with mud. Marco, Franco and Raphaeli lingered in the doorway while Bianca picked her way across to the cabinet where the paints should be and threw it open. Then her shoulders slumped.

'There's not enough paint to make a door,' she said. 'Cosimo and Lucia must've moved it all to di Lombardi's workshop – and we can't get there without a painted door.' *Another reason Franco cannot be allowed to ban us from using the passages*, Bianca thought sadly.

'We could go to Master Filpepi's studio?' Marco suggested weakly.

'I suppose we'll have to. But that'll cost us time, and who knows what's happening to Catriona while we run all over the city?' Bianca turned on the spot, opening drawers and cupboards, searching for anything at all that might help – until suddenly she saw something out of the corner of her eye. It was hidden at the back of a cupboard, covered in dust and not even upright – it seemed as if it'd slipped down there some time ago and never been found.

A small vial, half-full of *lux aurumque*.

'What've you found?' Marco asked. Bianca turned around and held up the vial.

139

'Can you make a door with that?' Secretary Franco asked.

'I can't make a whole painting with it,' Bianca said. 'What I *want* is . . .' She hesitated. 'I don't know, it might not even be possible.'

'*What?*' Marco asked.

'Well, if I could take this to an old-fashioned, ordinary painting, one that's completely non-magical, maybe I could do something that'd let me through. But it might not work, and anyway, where –'

'Mistress Frazetti,' chorused Marco and Captain Raphaeli. Bianca stared at them both, and then grinned.

Bianca and Marco hurried through the streets of La Luminosa just as dawn was breaking. The sunrise was as beautiful as ever, spears of bright light piercing pink and orange clouds, the sky above turning from pre-dawn pale blue to a deep, daylight blue.

Secretary Franco had found Mistress Frazetti's address in his records. She lived on the Via del Costello, a busy street between two canals. But today the city seemed strangely dim and quiet. There were people out on the wet, mud-caked streets – not the normal array of early-rising bakers and grocers and street sweepers, but bleary-eyed people from all walks of life who seemed uncertain what to do now that it was tomorrow, and they were at war. Most of them obviously hadn't been to sleep since they were woken by the water pouring out of the paintings and murals in their homes. There were so many magical paintings in the city that even some of the poorest families would have had a tiny magical sketch or a cameo for the water to leak out from.

And there were guards – *lots* of guards. Bianca couldn't help the urge to hide in the shadows and run to avoid them, even though she knew she hadn't done anything wrong. She self-consciously smoothed down her Oscuritan servant's outfit. She'd changed into it before they left the palace, and though it felt blessedly dry and warm after spending most of the night in a dress that'd been in the canal, she stuck out like a sore thumb amongst the bright colours and plain, pale cottons of La Luminosa.

On every street they saw guards with pails of black paint destroying the city's murals. More than once they passed carts laden with paintings, being driven slowly along by guards who stopped and knocked on every door they passed.

'Bring out any paintings you have inside,' one guard said to the frightened-looking old man who answered the door. 'Duchess Catriona's orders.'

The old man disappeared for a moment, and came back with a cracked painting of a young woman. She was laughing, her eyes bright. It was a magical painting. Bianca looked away and let Marco steer her quickly around a corner, afraid that if she caught the old man's eye he would know what she knew: his painting was too dangerous to leave alone, but not important enough to save. His laughing young lady would be thrown on the pyre.

Finally, they reached Mistress Frazetti's house. It was on one of the smaller canals, a large house set slightly apart from both its neighbours. A pair of servants were busily washing down the street outside, brushing the mud back into the canal with large brushes. They looked up in interest as Bianca and Marco walked up to the house and knocked on the door.

The door was opened just a crack and a young voice said, 'C-can I help you?'

'We need to see Mistress Frazetti,' Bianca said. From the sliver of her face she could see, the girl on the other side of the door only looked about their age, and she was shifting nervously from foot to foot. 'It's very, very important – it concerns the safety of the whole city,' Bianca said.

'I don't think so,' said the girl. 'No, thank you, we don't want any . . .'

'Maria, stand aside,' said another voice. The girl vanished and the door opened properly to reveal Mistress Frazetti herself. She looked rather different in her own home, fully dressed and with her thin grey hair pulled back into a bun at the nape of her neck. 'It *is* you,' she said. 'I thought I recognised your voice. And your gentlemanly companion,' she added, with a kindly smile at Marco. 'I cannot thank you enough for your help last night.'

'Mistress Frazetti, it's about last night we've come,' said Marco. 'It's about your painting.'

Mistress Frazetti's face took on a suspicious look. 'If you've come to burn my painting after all, I won't hear it,' she said.

'No, nothing like that,' Bianca said.

'Well,' said Marco, 'it's to do with all the trouble, with the water . . . It really would be easier to explain this inside,' he added.

'All right,' said Mistress Frazetti. She looked up and down the street before she waved them inside and locked the door behind them.

'Mistress Frazetti,' Bianca said, 'I would never ask this of you if it wasn't absolutely an emergency. The thing is, I need to use your painting. I need to . . . *alter* it, slightly.'

'Alter it?' the plump lady looked distinctly shocked. 'How? For what purpose?'

'I need to turn it into a magic painting, so I can use it to transport myself somewhere,' Bianca said, guessing that the truth was probably going to be just as convincing as any lie she could come up with.

Mistress Frazetti gazed at them for a moment. Then she smiled. 'Then you really are Master di Lombardi's granddaughter?'

Bianca blushed. She'd forgotten that she'd tried to pull rank on the guard who'd been trying to burn the painting. 'Well . . . yes,' she said.

'Well, I know you care more about art than anyone else in La Luminosa,' said Mistress Frazetti. 'I suppose if you want to alter my painting, you must have a good reason.'

'I do,' said Bianca. 'I promise.'

'All right,' said Mistress Frazetti. 'Follow me.'

She led them upstairs and into a room that had very little in it except for a big old wardrobe. Mistress Frazetti produced a key from her sleeve and unlocked the wardrobe.

'In case those guards come back,' she said. 'I'm not letting them get hold of this again.'

She opened the wardrobe and took out the painting. It

was about as tall as Bianca was from top to bottom.

'Who is she?' Marco asked, nodding at the little girl in the painting.

'My great-grandmother,' said Mistress Frazetti. 'A very good woman. Listen, dear – I hope this really is as important as you say it is.'

'It is, I promise,' said Bianca. 'And I promise not to do anything to hurt your great grandmother's portrait. I can work around her. If that's all right.'

Mistress Frazetti sighed. 'All right.'

'Great.' Bianca grinned with relief. 'Thank you, so much! Have you got any ink?'

'Oh, er – yes. It's in my study.'

'Will you get it?' Bianca asked Marco, kneeling in front of the painting and pulling out the vial of *lux aurumque* and di Lombardi's paintbrush. Marco gave her a little salute and then ushered Mistress Frazetti out of the room.

Bianca sighed, happy to be alone with the painting for a few minutes without its worried owner hovering over her shoulder. She touched the surface of the paint with careful fingers. It was painted with quite heavy strokes and thick layers of paint. That was good for Bianca. Even though it was a hundred years old, the paint might still respond to the *lux aurumque* when she painted it on. She might even be able to blend her doorway in seamlessly with the rest of the picture.

She uncorked the vial and dipped the brush into it. First, she needed to be able to get to the door, and that meant creating a pathway of real space from the foreground of the

144

painting to the background. She held the brush up, took a few deep breaths and tried to steady her own heartbeat.

She'd painted space into a picture before – but never one that was so old, or one that hadn't been designed with magic in mind. This was completely new territory.

Just like the first time you painted something solid, she thought. *Just like the time you made a door with nothing but* lux aurumque *petals and watercolours. You couldn't do it, and then you did.*

The thought was cheering. She began to paint, carefully skirting around the little girl, using the pressure of the brush to nudge and persuade the painting to take on magical properties and adapt to them, in the same way she'd use her thumb to make the first impressions on a piece of blank clay.

By the time Marco and Mistress Frazetti returned with an inkwell and a clean jar full of water, the whole left hand side of the picture had some depth to it.

Mistress Frazetti stood and stared at the painting.

'The tree looks so far away,' she muttered. 'It looks like you could walk right up to it.'

'Thank goodness,' said Bianca, reaching up and taking the ink. 'I need something to make a mark here, and I'm almost out of *lux aurumque*.' She dipped the paintbrush into the ink and reached into the painting. She heard Mistress Frazetti give a little gasp as she leaned into it and started to paint a shape onto the trunk of the big oak tree. Bianca was careful not to make too much of the black lines – just a subtle suggestion of darkness visible through the cracks in the bark, and two small holes chiselled into the wood to

145

serve as a keyhole and handle. Then she rinsed the brush and started to work over the lines with the golden, glowing fluid.

She pulled back, rinsed and wiped the brush again and then turned it in her hand.

'Hidden rooms, secret passages, second city,' she said.

'Oh, isn't that darling?' Mistress Frazetti said, staring hard at the small copper key as it clicked into place. 'But is this really going to work?'

Bianca didn't answer – the only answer she had was, *Oh God, I hope so.*

She leaned inside the painting, slid the key into the lock, turned it, and pulled on the door handle. The trunk of the tree swung out, almost as if it'd been designed that way from the beginning, and, beyond, Bianca saw the flickering torchlight, paint-speckled stone walls and puddle-strewn floor of the secret passages.

'We're in!' Marco said.

Bianca turned to the stunned lady and shook her hand gratefully. 'Thank you so much,' she said. 'Remind me to tell you what a great thing you've done for La Luminosa sometime.'

'All right,' said Marco. 'You ready?'

Bianca nodded. Then she grabbed him and gave him a big, squeezing hug. When she pulled away, he raised one eyebrow at her.

'I'm not coming, am I?'

Bianca shook her head. 'I'll do better by myself – I know my way around, and I know how to find the Resistance. I promise I'll be all right.'

'Be careful,' Marco said.

'I will.'

'More careful than that.'

Bianca fixed him with a serious stare and crossed her heart. 'I solemnly swear I will do absolutely everything I can not to get hurt. OK?'

'All right. Good luck,' Marco said, and stood back. Bianca smiled again at Mistress Frazetti, who was looking a little queasy, and then turned and climbed inside the painting.

It was a tight fit, because she hadn't had much canvas to work with, but the tree did grow a little bigger as she climbed through the painting towards it, and she ducked down and squeezed through the door in the trunk. When she was standing in the secret passages, she bent down and looked back, waving before shutting the door behind her.

Chapter Fifteen

As soon as she turned around and started walking down the passage, Bianca could tell that there was something wrong here. She could smell smoke, and the floor of the passage was still sloppy with canal water in wide puddles that Bianca had to hop and skip and criss-cross the corridor to avoid. She came to the end of a short passage, and looked both ways.

'This isn't right . . .' she muttered, and as soon as she'd said it she knew why. This *should've* been part of the passages that she knew, but some of the doors she had been expecting to see had just . . . gone. It was as if the doors on both sides of the missing ones had shifted up to take up the space, shortening the whole passage.

She walked up to the closest door and opened it a crack. She could see the inside of the painting. It was one she knew, with two girls dancing in front of a mirror. It should've been hanging in one of the guest rooms at the palace, but outside of the painting, there was nothing but a blank, white-ish void. It took her a moment to realise where she was: inside the stack of paintings that'd been moved to the museum. She reached out gingerly and prodded the white thing. She was right – it had the texture and give of canvas.

'This is odd,' she muttered, and pulled back into the passages, closing the door. She patted it, glad to know that this painting was safe, for now.

If that was the painting of the dancers, then Bianca thought the painting that led to the little walled garden in Oscurita ought to be to her left. She turned and started walking, hopping over or tiptoeing through the puddles, trying not to worry about the way the smell of smoke seemed to come and go.

A blast of heat and light from behind her made her skid on the wet floor, spinning around to see that one of the doors she'd just passed was on fire. There'd been no warning, no crackling or increase in heat, just a sudden burst of flame that roared over the surface of the door. Bianca stepped back, shielding her face, and watched as the fire crackled and flowed. There was a strong smell of burning paint – oil, bone, and a tang of magic that stung the back of Bianca's nose – and then the door crumbled to black ash.

Bianca blinked and rubbed her eyes. The door was gone and there was another in its place. She looked up and down the corridor. It had definitely become a little bit shorter.

Every painting that was destroyed made the secret passages smaller. If Secretary Franco ever destroyed them all, would the passages wink out of existence altogether? What would happen to someone who was in the passages when that happened? Or someone who tried to step through a door only to find it suddenly aflame?

She shuddered, and broke into a run. She had to get to

Oscurita, find her mother, find the Duchess, stop the war. *Then* she would handle Secretary Franco's terrible idea to ban all magical art.

The door to Oscurita was blessedly cool and solid under her hands when she eventually found it. Bianca opened it a tiny crack and looked through. The alleyway and neglected garden were empty. She climbed through the door and out into Oscurita without hesitating. She glanced back at the mural, with its cracked paint and subtle sense of depth. At least this one of her grandfather's works would be left alone.

Bianca realised she must be one of the very few in Oscurita who even knew it was an opening to the secret passages – Edita would have every entrance to La Luminosa that she knew about under guard, ready for the invasion.

She walked out through the archway to the street. She was heading for the big public square that she'd found by accident when she'd first visited Oscurita. At that time there had been barely any clue that this place was under the thumb of a tyrant. Everyone had seemed to be getting on with their normal lives, buying and selling from the market stalls that lined the streets, strolling along through the pools of crackling blue light from the thunder lamps in their glass orbs.

Straight away, this felt different. The streets were still full of people, perhaps even busier than before, but nobody strolled or stopped to chat – they walked quickly, clutching baskets or books to their chests, their hands thrust into the pockets of their black and grey frock coats and the hoods of their cloaks pulled up over their heads. A door along the street creaked open and then slammed shut again without anyone having stepped out.

There seemed to be fewer flashes of colour around their clothing too, though Bianca saw two women who looked like they belonged at Edita's court wearing long black velvet robes embroidered with bright purple and turquoise. They stopped walking and stood arm in arm, as if waiting for something. Then Bianca heard it – the sound of marching, armoured feet.

She looked around and saw a phalanx of soldiers coming towards her, armed to the teeth and carrying a purple banner.

Bianca's first thought was to run, but then she noticed that everybody else on the street had also stopped. They stared at their shoes or up to the starry sky. Nobody looked directly at the soldiers, but nobody turned their back on them either. A running figure among the crowd would be spotted at once, and chased down.

Bianca looked down at her feet, praying that her headdress and grey costume would protect her from being spotted.

The soldiers approached, drew level, and began to pass her. She swallowed hard as she counted the lines: five, ten, twenty rows of soldiers marching five abreast. A hundred soldiers – and that was just this troop. She sincerely doubted that this was the whole Oscuritan army.

None of them stopped to challenge her, or made any sound that suggested they'd even noticed her. The street seemed to come alive again after they'd passed by. Bianca let herself pause for a deep breath before she made herself join the hurrying crowd and cross the street. There was even more of an air of people scampering to get their business done and get home.

Bianca hurried through the dark streets, trying to look as if she was heading for an important errand and her mistress would miss her if she was stopped. She made it to the public square without being caught or questioned.

The square itself was almost deserted. When she'd been here before, it'd been as busy as the Piazza del Fiero, with stalls selling strange fruits and beautiful rolls of brightly coloured ribbon and thread. Now as she looked across at the statue of Annunzio di Lombardi, she gasped. The statue had been covered up, hastily draped with thick grey cloth and bound with rope. Bianca approached the statue, walking gingerly across the black and white tiles to the centre of the empty square. She felt a burst of anger when she saw that the *lux aurumque* flowers around the base of the plinth had all been cut down. Their black, stick-like stems poked up around the statue like a bed of thorns, but all their beautiful, glowing white flowers had been taken away.

A movement in the corner of Bianca's eye made her gasp, and she forced herself to turn around slowly, as if casually, to glance behind her.

A few people in heavy cloaks had entered the square and were walking quickly around the edge. One stopped to look at their reflection in the darkened window of a tavern. On an empty market stall nearby, a grey tabby cat licked its paws and gave Bianca a hard stare. Nothing else moved.

Bianca shook herself. She just had to keep moving. After all, there was nothing more suspicious than someone checking to see if they were followed every few minutes.

She stepped around the veiled statue and carried on across the square. Above her the spire of the Cathedral d'Oscurita loomed, black and spindly like one of the stems of the beheaded flowers. On the other side of the square, a few doors down from the cathedral's firmly shut doors, she saw it: Dante's Grocery. It was one of the very few shops in Oscurita that still seemed to be open – the windows glowed with the soft light of a fire in a hearth, and a lit thunder lamp hung over the door to illuminate the sign. There was even a woman coming out of the door carrying a small loaf of bread as Bianca approached. She gave Bianca a brief, appraising look, and then hurried off.

Bianca paused outside the shop, reading a sign that had been put up in one of the windows:

By order of the true Duchess Edita di Lombardi.
All citizens of Oscurita are henceforth placed under food
rations until the City of Light has been defeated and its
evil threat against our Oscurita has been ended.
Your support of our brave and noble soldier boys is appreciated.
Details and ration books available within.
ONE PER CITIZEN

Bianca raised her eyebrows at the sign. La Luminosa's evil threat against Oscurita? She would have laughed, if it hadn't been so ominous.

Could this be the place? It didn't look particularly revolutionary – and even more worryingly, the sign contained

153

the phrase 'the true Duchess Edita'. If she walked into this place and said 'God bless the true Duchess' as she'd been told, would the shopkeeper give her a blank look, or call the soldiers?

Still, the sign above the door said 'Dante's Grocery', and that was where Saralinda had told her to go. She had to trust her mother.

She screwed up her courage and pushed through the door and into the shop.

It seemed like a pretty ordinary grocer's shop. Apart from the everlasting darkness outside the window and the fire roaring in the hearth, and one or two strange fruits and vegetables in baskets by the door, it was just like the shop in La Luminosa where she used to go sometimes with Angela the kitchen maid to pick up a few extra ingredients for dinner.

'Got your ration book?' said a voice from the next room, making Bianca jump. 'Or are you here to pick one up?'

Bianca tried to breathe steadily and not look as scared as she felt when a large man in a leather apron appeared behind the counter. He had grey hair and a grey beard, and bags around his eyes as if he hadn't slept properly in a long time. To Bianca's surprise, he still wore a flash of colour on his dark grey tunic – a bright purple button over his heart in the shape of an open eye. It was small, but it shone out like a beacon in the dim shop.

'Are you Dante?' she asked.

The man frowned at her. 'The one and only,' he said, crossing his arms. She noticed that there were faded purple tattoos on his forearms. 'And what can I do for you?'

Bianca swallowed. It was now or never. She touched both eyes, her heart, and both her shoulders. 'God bless the true Duchess,' she said.

Without a word, Dante beckoned Bianca to come behind the counter, and then walked into a back room. Bianca clasped her hands together to try and stop them from shaking, glanced around to make sure there was nobody watching her through the windows from the square, and followed him.

She'd found the place.

'There it is,' said Dante, gesturing to the far wall of the storeroom.

Bianca frowned. There was no doorway, not even a painting – instead there was a big sculpture, a relief of the front of the cathedral.

'Um . . .' she said.

Dante's face broke into a friendly, conspiratorial smile and he walked up to the model and fished something that glinted out of his pocket. It was a key! He slipped it into the towering front doors of the cathedral – in real life they were several storeys high, and on the model they were just a little bit smaller than Bianca. They swung open and Bianca peered through to see a passage on the other side. It seemed to burrow straight through where the rest of the building should be, extending much further than it should.

'Is it magic?' Bianca asked.

Dante nodded and stood back to let Bianca go through, then bent nearly double and followed her inside, shutting the doors behind them.

'I didn't know you could make magical doors in sculptures too,' she said. 'I don't know why it never occurred to me.'

'This was created in a hurry,' said Dante. 'It goes only two places – my shop, and the hiding place of the Resistance. Don't be afraid,' he added. 'If you're the young lady I was told to expect, you're among friends.'

'I hope so,' Bianca muttered, as she followed him down the dark passage. There was a single torch halfway along the corridor. Bianca guessed that even for full-blooded Oscuritans, it gave only just enough light for them to navigate a straight line along the passage and not bash into the black stone walls. She reached out and let her fingers drag on the stone, and smiled as she realised that of course, this magical passage would feel as if it was chiselled out of stone, rather than painted onto canvas . . .

'You know, I helped your grandfather escape the palace so he could take you through to the bright city,' said Dante.

Bianca's heart rose at the mention of her grandfather.

'A real gent,' Dante continued. 'I was sorry to hear he died.'

'Thank you,' said Bianca.

'Now, remember what I said.' Dante unlocked and pushed open the doors at the other end. 'Don't be afraid.'

Bianca stepped through into what looked like some kind of vision of hell. She gasped and staggered back against the doors as Dante ducked through and shut them behind him. Skulls grinned at her from the walls, hundreds and hundreds of them, piled on top of each other like bricks, or tiles. A large candlestick in the middle of the room held twelve enormous red candles, casting flickering pink light over an altar made of rib cages and a snaking design across the ceiling that was laid out in hundreds of vertebrae. A whole, small skeleton stood to one side in a special alcove, which was also made of skulls. Its arms were crossed over its rib cage. Bianca forced herself to look closer, and saw the thin wires that'd been strung through the middle of the bones to hold them in that pose.

'Where have you brought me?' Bianca gasped.

'We're deep in the old catacombs of the city,' Dante said quietly. 'It's an Oscuritan tradition – instead of burial, people bequeathed their bones to the catacombs and the monks here made them into beautiful sculptures and decorations for their church. It's art.'

'It's . . . people!' Bianca squeaked.

'People who chose to be here,' said Dante, picking up a small candlestick that Bianca realised with a shudder was also made of bones. 'I'm thinking about asking to be laid down here when I go. Wouldn't you like to become part of something bigger and more beautiful than yourself when you die?'

Bianca wasn't sure what was more chilling: the fact that she was surrounded by the remains of hundreds and hundreds of corpses, or the fact that she could sort of see his point.

Dante led her through a series of chambers, each decorated in the same grim style – but after a few of the rooms, Bianca actually did begin to get used to it. Bizarrely, the severed skulls with their empty eye sockets and permanent chalky grins bothered her less than the rows and rows of tiny finger bones, or the occasional full-body skeleton dressed in monk's robes, looking for all the world as if it was just pausing to admire a skull-cave before getting on with its daily rituals.

Bianca did yelp and grab onto Dante's arm as she saw something move in a chamber they'd just left. When Dante agreed to look into the room, he shook his head. 'Nothing,' he said, shining his candle on the hooded monk figure in one corner, the piles of skulls and the ceiling decoration made out of broken bone shards arranged like a mosaic. 'Could be the rats, but they won't bother you. They've got busy little ratty lives.'

Bianca wished she hadn't asked.

'Now, this gives me the creeps,' said Dante as they walked into the next chamber.

There was no light in the room apart from Dante's single red candle. He held it up so Bianca could get a better view of the rows of marble statues – each one exactly the same, each one showing Duchess Edita with an odd smile on her face, reaching out for Bianca with one hand. Bianca jumped and cringed away from them, but they didn't move. They were just statues.

Bianca made herself approach the nearest one, and as she did shards of marble crunched under her feet. She touched the end of one of the statues' hands.

'The fingers have partly broken off,' she said. She looked at the next one – it was the same, but missing a whole hand. The next one was different – what looked like part of a marble sleeve was still attached to the end of the fingers.

Bianca felt a chill run down her spine that had nothing to do with the cold air in the catacombs. She moved around to look at the statues from side on, and shook her head. 'That's so weird,' she muttered. 'It's the exact same statue the Baron gave to Duchess Catriona in the garden – but whoever was being embraced in each of these, they've vanished. Like they've all been smashed.'

'Come on,' said Dante, holding open a door on the other side of the room. 'I don't like to be in here too long.'

Bianca had to agree. She followed him through the door and found herself in a large chamber, brightly lit – for Oscurita, anyway – with white candles and thunder lamps, and occupied by six or seven men and women in simple grey and black clothes. Each of them was heavily armed, with swords and daggers at their belts.

And standing at a table in the middle of the room, deep in conversation with Pietro over a pile of documents, was Saralinda.

Bianca felt as if a heavy cloak she hadn't realised she'd been wearing had been pulled away.

Saralinda looked up and saw Bianca, and her eyes widened. Bianca took a few steps across the room, beginning to smile, trying to restrain herself from simply rushing into her mother's arms.

But Saralinda frowned. She stepped away from the table, shaking her head. 'Bianca! What are you doing here?'

Bianca's steps faltered and stopped. The Resistance all turned to stare at her. A few of them muttered to each other.

'You cannot be here,' Saralinda went on. 'Didn't I tell you not to come? You are the last hope of the Resistance. If something were to happen to me you would be the only person who could get rid of Edita. You have *got* to take that seriously!'

'I do,' said Bianca in a small voice. 'It's an emergency!'

'Oh darling, I'm sure it is. Come here,' said Saralinda, and she walked over to Bianca and opened her arms. Bianca rushed into them and embraced her mother tightly. 'You know I'm happy to see you,' Saralinda said. 'Always. I'm just so worried for you.'

'I'm fine,' said Bianca. 'It's Duchess Catriona who's in trouble. She's vanished from La Luminosa.'

'What?' Saralinda gasped. 'We didn't know that. Are *you* all right? Did you manage to stop the flood?'

Bianca nodded. 'It caused chaos in La Luminosa. They're . . . they're burning lots of the magical paintings, and locking the rest away. If Marco and I hadn't seen the Baron drop his talisman in the canal . . . I don't want to think about what would've happened.'

'I'm so sorry,' Saralinda said. 'I tried to stop it when I heard what was happening to you, but we couldn't do anything to fix it from here.'

'Duchess Catriona smashed the talisman. And then she vanished from her bedchamber. There was no sign of her, and nowhere she could have gone, just another talisman – a white marble medallion. We thought the Baron must have magicked her back here.' Bianca hesitated, not at all liking the blank look on her mother's face.

'Pietro?' Saralinda asked, turning to the Resistance leader. 'Have you heard anything about the Duchess being brought to the castle, or kept somewhere in secret?'

Pietro shook his head. 'I'm sorry, Lady Bianca. We have spies all over the castle now that we're getting ready to make our move, but I haven't heard anything about Duchess Catriona being brought to Oscurita.'

'We saw the Baron and his delegation coming back,' volunteered another Resistance fighter, a woman with pale blonde hair cropped close to her head. 'We've got people watching all the entrances to the city. Belladonna's hardly taken her eyes off the Baron for a second since he got back,' she said, mostly to Pietro, who nodded. 'We'd know if he had Catriona hidden somewhere.'

'But if she's not here,' Bianca said, 'where has she gone? I can't go home without some answers!'

'I'm so sorry,' said Saralinda gently, pulling Bianca into another hug. 'I don't know.'

Bianca took a deep breath. 'Thanks,' she said. 'I'm sorry I had to come here for nothing.'

'Well,' Saralinda pulled away and smiled at Bianca. 'Not quite nothing. I actually have something for you.' She beckoned Bianca over to one of the skull-covered alcoves. Bianca gave a small shudder as she realised that this was where her mother was sleeping. There was a bed made of rolled-up blankets and cushions, and on it were a sharp-looking stiletto dagger, and a sealed envelope. Saralinda picked up the envelope and held it tight for a moment, before handing it to Bianca.

'What is it?' Bianca asked. 'Can I open it?'

'Not now,' said Saralinda. 'Keep it safe and open it when you get home to La Luminosa. It's . . . Bianca, you know I haven't been able to tell you who your father is,' she said quietly. Bianca blinked down at the envelope and nodded. 'I don't know where he is now – and he never knew my real identity. I just can't find the words to talk about it. So . . . I've made you this. It will tell you everything.'

Bianca sucked in a deep breath. 'Thank you,' she said softly. 'Thank you so much. But I would love you to tell me. In your own words.' Bianca folded the envelope away in her pocket and stared into her mother's glistening blue eyes.

Saralinda raised a hand and stroked Bianca's hair back off her face. 'I could try, I suppose.'

There was a *bang* that seemed to rattle the bones on the walls and the door to the chamber burst open. A figure stepped through in a hooded cloak that swept around him as he raised his arm. The Resistance fighters yelled and drew their swords. The arm was holding a crossbow. Saralinda shoved Bianca down, hard, and she fell to the floor. The cold stone slammed into her hands and knees, and she looked up, under the man's hood, and saw the face of the artist, Filpepi. His eyes flickered to her, widened with triumph, and the crossbow bolt shot from the bow and ripped through the air over Bianca's head.

A second later Filpepi was down, wrestled to the floor by Resistance fighters. The blonde woman pressed her dagger to his throat and he stopped struggling.

Bianca sat up, bracing herself for a barrage of Oscuritan guards pouring through the door – but there were none.

'How did you find us?' the woman growled. 'Answer, scum!'

Filpepi let out a gurgling laugh, and pointed. His finger landed squarely on Bianca. 'I'd recognise the face of my old *apprentice* anywhere. I didn't have time to call reinforcements before I followed you, Bianca. But it doesn't matter. Now . . . it's all over for your little rebellion . . .' he hissed.

'Saralinda!' Pietro gasped.

Bianca turned around and saw her mother, leaning against the wall of skulls, blood cascading from the crossbow bolt that protruded from her chest.

'Mother!' Bianca screamed, and tried to get to Saralinda, but somebody grabbed her and pulled her back.

Saralinda made a gurgling sound and slid down to the floor, leaving a trail of red across the bleached white bone behind her.

Bianca struggled and scratched. She *had* to get to her mother. She *had* to save her.

Pietro and the rest of the Resistance rushed to Saralinda's side and carefully moved her so she was lying down on the bed. Bianca went limp against the arms that held her as she watched one of the Resistance staunch the bleeding.

'Let them work,' said Dante, giving her a squeeze and then releasing her, but keeping a steadying hand on her shoulder. 'They'll do everything they can.'

'Get Lady Bianca out of here,' Pietro said, turning to Dante. 'Get her back to La Luminosa, right now.'

'I won't leave her,' Bianca tried to say, her throat closing over the final words. She gave a huge, shuddering sob.

'You must,' said Pietro, pulling away from her mother to kneel in front of her. He grabbed her hands and made her look at him. 'If this . . . goes badly,' he said, and his eyes glittered with tears, 'you are Oscurita's only hope.'

'Bianca . . .' Saralinda called out, weakly, from behind the crowd of Resistance fighters struggling to help her. 'Run.'

Chapter Sixteen

Bianca came to suddenly and sat up, disoriented. Where was she? There was sunlight on her face. She'd had terrible dreams that seemed to grasp at her and try to suck her back under – dreams of drowning, in a dark passage surrounded by nothing but bones . . .

'Bianca! You're awake!'

She blinked, and everything swam into focus. She was in her own bed, in the palace, in La Luminosa, and Marco was sitting up in a chair beside the bed.

'What happened?' she asked him. She remembered Dante helping her into the passages and she remembered telling him that she would be able to make it back to La Luminosa by herself. She didn't remember how she'd found her way back to the painting in Mistress Frazetti's house.

'You came out of the painting at a run, and fainted,' Marco said. 'You were out for a couple of hours. Did you find the Duchess?'

She remembered the crossbow sticking out of her mother's chest.

'No, I . . .'

Her mother was wounded, maybe . . . dead.

She leapt out of bed. Marco cried 'Hey, careful!' and jumped up, just in time to steady her shoulders as the world swam around her head.

'I've got to go,' she said. 'I've got to tell Raphaeli what happened.'

'You're not running off like this – you've been unconscious nearly all day!'

'You don't understand, I've got to . . . My mother . . .' She fought to push down the tears, but it was no use. Her knees buckled and she sank to the floor. Marco knelt beside her and she tried to wipe her tears away on the silky blanket, but it was no use. She curled up tight and cried until she felt as if she'd cried herself inside out.

'What happened to Saralinda?' Marco whispered.

'She was shot,' Bianca gasped. 'Filpepi followed me through the secret entrance, and . . . and . . .' She fought to get a hold of herself. Marco put his arms around Bianca's shoulders and hugged her tight.

Bianca had always thought she was an orphan, a foundling left on Master di Lombardi's doorstep. Not having parents had never hurt her before. It wasn't until she'd found her mother that it hurt to think about losing her again . . .

Marco let Bianca go, stood up, and then knelt down again with something in his hands – a white envelope.

'What's this?' he asked.

'I don't have time for that now,' Bianca said. She tried to get to her feet again, but found herself sitting on the edge of the bed. 'I've got to tell Raphaeli that the Duchess is still here.'

'Catriona's in La Luminosa?'

'That's what my mother said . . . she said if she'd been brought into Oscurita she'd know.'

'All right. Tell you what. You open the letter, I'll go and tell Raphaeli.'

Bianca gave Marco a suspicious look. 'You're just trying to get me to sit still for a bit longer,' she said.

'Fine, you saw through my cunning plan. You can run around as much as you like as soon as you can honestly say you won't fall on your face,' Marco said, pointedly placing the envelope in Bianca's hands. He stood up and moved towards the door.

'Marco?' Bianca said, wiping her eyes on her sleeve. Marco turned. 'Thanks.'

Bianca stared down at the envelope, as Marco's quick footsteps echoed away down the corridor. The answers to all her questions about her father were inside, but they suddenly didn't seem important now that her mother could be lying dead in Oscurita, perhaps buried in some secret funeral – a funeral that she could never attend. After all this, did she really want to know who her father was? What if he was already dead, too? Or if he'd left the city and she would never find him?

No, of course she had to know.

She opened the envelope. It contained a small scrap of paper and a larger, folded sheet of thick parchment.

Bianca read the note first.

167

Dearest Bianca,

*I can't express how glad I am to have the chance
to know you. I think that your father, if you find
him, will feel the same. Know that I loved him
very deeply, and he felt the same about me. We
were torn apart when Edita seized the throne and
I had to return to Oscurita.*

*We can talk all of this through properly when
we can finally be together, for good.*

*Your loving mother,
Saralinda*

Bianca put the note down. She felt almost faint with the knowledge that that might never happen.

Taking a deep breath, she unfolded the parchment.

There was a picture painted on the parchment, a simple line drawing in blue paint. It was a picture of Saralinda, though she looked much younger, perhaps nineteen or twenty.

Bianca almost dropped the parchment as the young Saralinda turned, smiled, and the perspective of the picture shifted to show her standing in a doorway, her hands held nervously in front of her, wearing a simple dress and carrying an easel.

It was a *storia*. The same magical, animated painting that her grandfather had left to her to explain the story of how he had escaped Oscurita with her as a baby. But this one showed a different story. . .

It was night time, and Saralinda – in disguise as her

father's apprentice – was standing near the back of a group of Oscuritan nobles as they were introduced into the throne room of La Luminosa. The pictures followed Saralinda as she approached the throne and curtseyed to the Duke. He gave her a smile that was so sad it hurt Bianca to look at it. But then his eyes lit up as something tugged on his sleeve and a toddler climbed into his lap. Bianca couldn't help but smile as the baby Catriona chewed on the Duke's sceptre and demanded to be bounced on his knee.

Oh, Catriona. Where are you now? Please be all right . . .

The Duke kissed Saralinda's hand, and the scene abruptly swam and changed.

Now, Saralinda was wearing a fine dress and a simple mask with the face of a cat. She was at a masquerade ball. Exquisite costumes flashed past her in the background. Saralinda looked around, as if searching for somebody. In the next picture, she was dancing with a man, and they were both laughing. His mask was a simple bird shape, with a protruding beak and a wide-brimmed hat. The ball passed in a series of glimpses, of moments. The bird-man held her hand. They sat together on a bench outside the ballroom, looking at the stars. She bent down to pick up his mask, which had dropped to the ground . . . and she gasped.

It wasn't the Duke. Saralinda ran from him, and he went after her, into the gardens. Bianca strained to see the man's face, but the picture moved too quickly. But he had long, curly hair that had been hidden under his hat until now. It definitely wasn't the Duke. Saralinda began speaking to him, holding his hands, shaking her head . . . and then somehow she was laughing. Saralinda and the bird-man embraced, and then kissed.

The scene changed again – a darkened chapel, empty but for three figures: Saralinda and Bianca's father, exchanging rings, in front of an elderly priest. Bianca let out a tiny, happy sound. Her parents had been secretly married! Saralinda was wearing her plain apprentice's clothes, and Bianca's father was in a simple doublet with a sword at his belt. It was so romantic, it made her heart hurt.

Another scene: the Duke and Saralinda, deep in conversation. The Duke listened as Saralinda talked. She showed him her ring. The Duke smiled and shook Saralinda's hands. He shook his head and his smile widened. He looked . . . relieved. He must never have truly wanted to remarry, Bianca thought. Her mother must have saved him from having to choose between his own heart and the good of his country . . .

And then, suddenly, Saralinda looked up. Joy and sadness mingled in Bianca's heart as she saw her grandfather, Annunzio di Lombardi, enter the room with a grim and worried face. He said something to Saralinda and her smile vanished. The Duke bowed to them and they both ran out of the room.

The final scene showed Saralinda, standing in the doorway of a painting, looking down at the ring on her hand, and then closing the door behind her.

The parchment went blank. Bianca sat back with a sigh.

It was so wonderful to know, finally, what had happened. How her mother and father had met, and how they'd been torn apart. But her father . . . who *was* he? One of the nobles? Several of them had very curly hair, but none of them seemed to fit the glimpses the *storia* had given her of the man's face.

Suddenly, the paint on the parchment welled up again, settling in the form of one final picture. A large and detailed painting of the rings her mother and father had exchanged. They were strong, simple bands with only one decoration: matching engravings of trailing ivy that wound around the inside and the outside of the rings.

Bianca drew back a little from the parchment, her heart beating faster.

That ring – she'd seen it before. She'd seen one just like it. But where? She shut her eyes, seeing it dangling in front of her, catching the light . . .

Bianca opened her eyes and stared at nothing for a moment.

'Captain Raphaeli,' she whispered.

He had definitely had a ring just like the one on the parchment in front of her. He'd told her, that same day, he knew that good and bad people came from Oscurita. He'd even said he was there when some people had come through the paintings in the Duke's time.

Bianca frowned. Wouldn't he have said something, when she was talking about visiting Oscurita? She'd mentioned enough times that her mother was Saralinda, the true Duchess.

But then, he had never known who she really was. Saralinda had told her that.

But, he knew she was from Oscurita, and he'd wanted to destroy all the paintings! How could he have done that, if he knew it was the only way he might one day be reunited with the woman he supposedly loved? He'd certainly loved her enough to marry her in secret, and to keep her ring with him even twelve years later . . .

Bianca shook her head. She was going around in circles. She would just have to find Raphaeli and make him talk to her. She would ask him outright – it was the only sensible way to get to the truth. If it wasn't him, or he'd found the ring somewhere, or he didn't want to know her or see her mother again . . . at least she would know.

There was a cry down in the courtyard, words Bianca couldn't quite make out, and then the sound of running feet and a clatter of metal. She leapt to her feet, and almost collided with the maid as she pushed the door open.

'Oh! Lady Bianca,' she said. Her face was drawn and she looked scared. She bobbed a very short curtsey.

'What's going on?' Bianca asked, afraid she already knew the answer.

'My Lady, you have to come. The Dark City has started an invasion. We're under attack!'

Chapter Seventeen

The streets of La Luminosa were bright with lamps and torches and crowded with people as Bianca ran past. She overtook a phalanx of guards in shining armour and a ragtag bunch of volunteers wearing whatever protective clothing they could get their hands on – leather blacksmith's aprons, stiff woollen cloaks, ancient and rusty chainmail. They carried old axes, boat oars and butcher's knives.

'Unarmed citizens are to take to the canals,' cried a young page on a street corner as Bianca sprinted past. He was pointing a frightened-looking man holding two small children towards a boat moored up nearby. 'The boats will take you across the bay to San Marino. You'll be safe on the island as long as we hold the city.'

There was a metallic clanging and Bianca had to dodge out of the way as the crowd in front of her parted to reveal an old woman hitting a frying pan with a wooden spoon, yelling, 'Knives sharpened here!' She was standing next to an even older man who was bent over a knife-sharpening wheel, grinding an axe until its blunt edges looked deadly once again.

There was a quiet roar of nervous chatter, orders being passed along, children crying and tearful farewells-for-now, but Bianca didn't hear any actual sounds of battle. Yet.

'Cavalry go around by the Via del Luce!' One guard just outside the Museum Piazza was standing on a pile of boxes, directing the forces. 'Pikemen and spears to the front, let them through! Swords, knives and clubs go around to the right and await orders from Lieutenant Forza.' He took off his helmet and Bianca saw that he was young, barely older than Cosimo. He took a deep breath, shoved his helmet back on his head, and yelled out, 'God bless the Duchess!'

'God bless the Duchess!' the crowd replied. 'God bless Her Highness!'

Bianca stopped in her tracks, feeling sick. There was still no Duchess – nobody to lead La Luminosa into battle. Bianca had failed to find her.

As soon as Bianca entered the Museum Piazza, she heard the banging. It was coming from inside the museum. She slipped easily through the lines of soldiers and volunteers and climbed up onto the fountain in the middle of the piazza. The museum doors and windows had all been boarded up with thick, heavy oak boards – some of them were water-worn and Bianca wondered if they'd been torn out from the docks. The boards rattled and brick dust flew out in clouds as the Oscuritan forces inside the museum bashed at the doors – trying to get out and attack.

The army that was coming through the paintings was surrounded, penned in inside the museum – but Bianca feared that wouldn't hold them for long. They still badly outnumbered the La Luminosan army. More Oscuritan soldiers could simply keep pouring through until they were overwhelmed.

In front of the building, Captain Raphaeli gleamed in his full golden plate armour. He was riding an enormous brown horse that was almost as armoured as he was. He trotted along the front line of the La Luminosan defence, his helmet under his arm, calling out orders and encouragement to his subordinates.

Bianca stared at him – his slightly beak-like nose, his noble bearing, and his thick curly hair.

Captain Raphaeli was her father. There was no more doubt in her mind. Even without a clear picture of his face, he was unmistakeably the man in the *storia* her mother had painted.

Bianca's heart lurched. How could she tell him?

I'm your daughter. You're my father. The woman you married twelve years ago in secret is my mother . . . and she's the rightful Duchess of Oscurita . . .

The museum doors splintered, and the La Luminosan forces visibly recoiled, all of the volunteers and several of the soldiers taking half a step back.

'Stand your ground!' Captain Raphaeli shouted, turning his horse and drawing his sword. 'Defend your homes!'

'Captain, why don't we burn the museum?' asked one of the young soldiers nearby. 'We've got them trapped!'

'No,' snapped Captain Raphaeli. 'After everything I've gone through to save the art in there, I won't burn it all now!' Bianca's heart swelled. 'Anyway, the doors will be the first thing to burn, and then we definitely won't be able to contain them. We have them surrounded, there's nowhere they can go.'

Bianca jumped down from the fountain and sprinted through the crowd to the front line. Scraping her hair back from her face, she realised she shouldn't tell him anything now. She couldn't tell him that she was his daughter, and his wife was probably dead, and that she was responsible. Perhaps it would be better for him never to know, never to have his heart awakened and then broken in two.

Still, she had to say *something* to him.

'Captain!' she shouted. 'Captain Raphaeli!'

Raphaeli looked down, and his face drained of colour for a moment. 'Bianca! Lady Bianca, what are you doing? You can't be here – this is a battlefield!'

Bianca ran up to him and grabbed the reins of his horse. She looked up at him, and then spoke quickly and quietly. 'I . . . I'm so sorry. I couldn't find the Duchess. My mother hadn't heard anything about her being brought to Oscurita. She said she's probably hidden in La Luminosa. And then . . . then . . .' She couldn't do it. 'I don't know how to find her. I'm so sorry.'

'None of this is your fault,' Raphaeli said. 'It's because of you we even have this number of fighters. If you hadn't warned us when the passages first reopened, we'd be overwhelmed.' He shook his head. 'If only we'd had more time to train some of these volunteers. They don't know how to follow orders – they'll just listen to whoever shouts loudest.'

'It should be the Duchess leading them into battle,' said Bianca.

176

'You're right.' Captain Raphaeli's horse danced a few steps away as the Oscuritans bashed into the museum doors again. Raphaeli didn't blink. 'I hate the idea of her fighting in battle, but she'd be worth twenty soldiers if she was here. I had some people climb up to the high windows on the museum and look inside. Edita's in there on a black charger, and her people are clearly rallied around her.'

'Is it . . . is it hopeless?' Bianca asked.

'Nothing is hopeless,' Captain Raphaeli said firmly. 'But I'd give my right arm for a hundred more soldiers,' he added. 'Or for Duchess Catriona to be here. Even Filpepi's painted doll would do! The people need to see what they're fighting for.'

An idea hit Bianca so hard she almost rocked back on her heels from the force of it. 'Filpepi's painted Duchess . . .' she breathed. She looked up at the Captain – at her father – and forced a smile. 'I think I have a plan,' she said.

'Be careful, Bianca!' Captain Raphaeli called after her as she turned and ran off. 'Keep away from the fighting!'

Bianca hurried out of the crowd and out of the piazza, pausing as she passed the young guard who was still giving orders to new arrivals. She caught her breath and stared up at the stars, trying to think her plan through.

If Filpepi can bring paintings to life, I can too. I can make new soldiers.

But it was all very well to know that it was *possible*. She had to be practical. The best supply of paint and tools was, by far, di Lombardi's secret workshop. But how could she get there? All the paintings were in the museum, and even if she could

177

get into the passages, they would be swarming with Oscuritan soldiers. She could fly in through the skylight, if she sprouted wings – the flying machine was still inside the studio.

'Bianca!' That was Marco's voice. Bianca looked around, unable to see him at first, until suddenly the crowd parted and she spotted him waving at her. She ran over.

He was standing with his father, Master Xavier, who was carrying his big wooden staff with the round orb on the end. Bianca had never quite noticed how heavy it looked before, or how easily it could be used as a club. Most of the rest of the troupe were there too – Olivia was wearing silver-painted wooden costume armour and carrying a prop scimitar that'd been sharpened until its edge glinted, and Bianca saw the fire twins, Carmina and Valentino, and half a dozen others wielding weapons that looked like they'd been cobbled together from props and bits of staging.

'Bianca, there you are,' said Cosimo. Bianca turned to see him standing beside the tumblers. Behind him stood Lucia, Ezio, Gennaro and Rosa. They were rather worryingly well armed with palette knives, hammers, chisels and shears.

'Where are the other apprentices? Are they safe?'

'They've gone to the island,' Lucia said. 'And that's where you need to go too!'

'I agree,' said Master Xavier. He looked down at Marco with a mixture of pride and abject terror. 'And please take my son with you – by force, if necessary.'

'I told you,' Marco said firmly, 'I have to help protect the city!'

'Actually, I do want Marco,' Bianca said. 'Marco, where's the underwater craft?'

178

'Still moored up by the Bridge of Cats,' said Marco.

'Can we use it to get into the secret workshop?'

Marco's face lit up. 'Yes! We can go in through the trapdoor into the canal!'

'We need to go, right now – I'll explain later.'

Master Xavier still looked concerned. 'Just be careful in that thing. Despite what Marco tells me, being stuck in a sealed vessel at the bottom of a canal doesn't sound safe.'

He and Olivia gathered Marco into a tight three-way hug. Bianca ran forward and gave each of the apprentices a huge hug in turn – even Lucia – although she saved her hardest squeeze for Cosimo.

'Good luck,' she said.

She grabbed Marco's hand and dragged him back down the street towards the Bridge of Cats.

'What are you going to do?' Marco asked, running the length of di Lombardi's workshop with an armful of more wicked-looking tools that could be used as weapons, and loading them into the underwater craft.

Bianca was mixing paints frantically, creating the strongest *animare* she could. She already had two large jars of glowing liquid that sloshed and jumped around the jars with a mind of its own, but she had a feeling there was something missing.

'I can't paint a whole army,' she muttered. 'To paint a soldier that's convincing enough for the *animare* to lift it off the page – I don't have that kind of time. And even if I could get the painted men out of the painting, they'd only be able to follow moves I made with the brush.'

Bianca almost dropped her paintbrush as a mad idea flashed into her mind.

'Marco,' she said softly. Marco looked up. 'I'm going to do something a little bit mad. It might be dangerous. I . . . have no idea if I can undo it.'

'You're going to make soldiers out of paint!' Marco cried.

'Not paint . . . Sculptures.'

Marco look confused. Then, when he realised what she meant, his dark eyebrows lowered in a questioning frown.

'You *can* enchant sculptures. I've seen it in Oscurita!' Bianca said, seeing his expression. She walked, slowly, back over to the paint-mixing bench and looked at her three batches of *animare*, swirling in their jars. Then she found a sharp scalpel and pushed it into the top of her finger. She winced as she felt a sharp pain, and her finger started bleeding.

Bianca gingerly unscrewed the lids from the *animare* pots and one by one she added a single drop of her own blood to the mixture. The *animare* leapt, spat, and gave off a piercing bright blue light.

'Woah,' said Marco. 'Let's try it!' He grabbed a small clay statue of an angel, about the length of Bianca's forearm – a study for a larger version, Bianca thought – and ran over to her table with it. Bianca dipped her brush in the violently churning *animare* and then touched it to the angel's forehead.

A shimmer ran over the clay and the angel beat its wings and blinked. It looked around, as if puzzled to find itself suddenly alive.

'Can . . . can you understand me?' Bianca said.

The angel folded its arms and nodded.

'*OhmyGoditworked!*' Bianca yelled.

The angel tilted its head to the side, but continued to stare intently at Bianca.

'The city's under threat,' she told the little figurine. 'We need you to fight. Can you do that?'

The angel hopped down off its plinth and shook the extra clay off its feet. Then it leapt into the air and flapped across the workshop to the clay-sculpting bench, where it grabbed a chisel almost as big as itself and held it like a spear.

'Marco, load up the jars!' Bianca grinned, quickly retrieving a small vial and pouring in a portion of the dancing blue *animare* for herself. Clutching the glass container in one fist, she ran over to the lever on the wall that controlled the opening and closing of the skylight windows. Grabbing the handle, she winched it round and round until the window was open far enough for the angel to get out. 'We'll meet you there!' she called back to Marco, as the clay sculpture shot up through the gap and vanished into the starry sky.

Chapter Eighteen

'Are we in time?' Bianca asked, clinging onto the stone fur of the great black panther as it bounded through the streets, its huge marble paws striking the cobbles with a chorus of *thunks*. 'Has the battle started?'

'I think we made it!' Marco said, peering around General Negra's stone shoulder as her stone horse drew level with Bianca's big cat.

Ahead of them the crowd of soldiers and volunteers turned, looked back, and parted with a chorus of gasps. Several of the soldiers swore, loudly and imaginatively, and comments of 'What on earth is that?' spread quickly as they took in the sight. The two enormous panthers from the Bridge of Cats led the pack, with General Negra and a whole troop of warlike statues of soldiers just behind. The old god of the sea lumbered after them, looking distinctly grumpy, still dripping with mud from the canal bed and with one shoe dangling from his enormous stone trident. There was a pack of stone dogs of all shapes and sizes running at his heels, and bringing up the rear, a whole flying phalanx of angels – some from grand houses and public buildings, some from the palace gardens, with their golden swords glinting in the starlight, and some with tear-streaked faces from the city cemetery. Finally, the little cat-sized dragons from the Piazza del Fiero zoomed through the air behind the angels, roaring in voices like stones grating together and trying to breathe fire.

Bianca grinned to herself as the panther led the procession of statues towards the Museum of Art. The doors were still holding, but only barely – a gang of soldiers were holding them shut, using the barriers that'd been knocked down as braces.

Captain Raphaeli looked up, saw Bianca's reinforcements, and his jaw fell.

'Can they fight?' he asked Bianca after a second.

'Yes, sir,' she said. She hopped down from the panther and ran towards the museum doors.

'What are you doing now?' Raphaeli demanded.

'Two more recruits, sir!' Bianca grinned. She whipped out the small vial of *animare*, as well as a thick-haired paintbrush from her pocket. Dipping the brush into the glass container, she soaked up the whole portion of magical blue liquid, before daubing it on the forehead of each of the enormous stone lions that stood on either side of the museum entrance. The soldiers saw them come to life and almost let go of the door, but Raphaeli yelled at them and they managed to hold fast, even when one of the lions sat back on its haunches and dragged a stone tongue over its stone paw.

Captain Raphaeli turned to Bianca.

'You', he said, 'are a truly inspirational young lady.'

Bianca beamed up at her father. Then she turned to Marco. 'C'mon,' she said, 'we're more use searching for more statues to recruit than standing here.' Marco nodded his agreement and slid down from Negra's horse.

And then there was a great splintering and tearing. The doors to the museum finally cracked apart. A terrifying shout of triumph erupted from inside the museum. The La Luminosan soldiers jumped out of the way as the doors collapsed out onto the street.

Raphaeli drew his sword and wheeled his horse around. 'For the Duchess!' he cried. 'For La Luminosa!'

A great cheer went up from the soldiers all around them, and then the Oscuritan soldiers were surging out from the museum just like the water that had poured from the enchanted paintings. The sound of spear clashing on spear and the screams and the roars of triumph and despair that rose from the soldiers were almost unbearable. Bianca staggered back, her own fear hitting her far harder than she'd expected. She saw her first soldier fall – an Oscuritan. He hit the ground face down and blood ran between the cracks in the stones of the piazza.

Bianca turned and tried to sprint back through the crowd of soldiers. She had to get to the rest of the *animare*, then she could make more statue reinforcements and give La Luminosa an even better chance. But someone caught her by the shoulder and she tripped. She looked up into the shiny silver helmet of an Oscuritan soldier. He raised his spear, ready to run her through, and then there was a *clong* as the stone hooves of General Negra's horse connected with his helmet. The soldier fell back and Bianca scrambled to her feet.

Oscuritan soldiers were all around her, fighting with the La Luminosan soldiers. She saw an Oscuritan sword flash as it ran through an old man wielding a boathook. She looked away and saw two of the stone soldiers she'd awakened, fighting back to back against a whole troop of Oscuritan soldiers. Stone chips flew off the statues as the Oscuritan spears and swords hit them, but they kept on fighting.

Bianca picked herself up and tried to slip away again. The soldiers flowed back and forth like a tide and an undertow, fighting against one another and spinning her around. She didn't know where Marco was, or Raphaeli. Her hands shaking, she made a grab for a shield that'd been dropped and picked it up. She didn't feel any safer. All around her there were yells of pain and fear.

There was a sound of hooves on the stone and Bianca looked up to see Edita's black charger stomping and snorting, rearing and kicking out at soldiers who got too close. Edita herself was wielding a mace that looked like it could take someone's head right off. She slammed it into the back of one of the statues of a La Luminosan soldier. The statue splintered and shattered into stone chunks. Edita wheeled the mace around and brought it down on something Bianca couldn't see. It made a sickening *crunch*.

But Edita hadn't seen Bianca – and she didn't see the marble angels that swept out of the air and knocked her off balance. The weight of the mace itself dragged her down and she slid off the horse and vanished into the melee.

Bianca forced herself to move. She crouched behind the shield and hobbled slowly across the piazza. As she reached the fountain, she heard Captain Raphaeli's voice calling out orders and felt a rush of relief. He was still alive. She pressed herself back against the fountain's base as the La Luminosan cavalry stormed into the piazza, the horses' hooves thundering on the cobbles. Bianca looked around again for Marco, imagining him dying any number of terrible deaths in the chaos of battle. She couldn't see him, and she couldn't just stand here and wait for him either.

Got to get to where I can be useful.

She climbed up on the fountain, searching the piazza for a route out. She spotted the old god, towering above the other fighters, smashing Oscuritan soldiers with his enormous fists – then ropes were looped around his head and neck and he lost balance and crashed to the ground with a noise like a demolished building.

From her vantage point, she could see more clearly than ever that the La Luminosans were horribly outnumbered.

Bianca hopped down from the fountain and slipped between the fighters.

Just for a moment, a path opened up before her – a clear corridor. She could see the street leading away from the piazza. Down there, the underwater craft was moored. The last of the *animare* was there. If she could just –

A dark figure stepped into her path.

'Dearest niece,' snarled Duchess Edita, and swung her mace. Bianca threw herself backwards and raised the shield just in time. Edita's mace glanced off it. Bianca yelped with pain – the mace had barely scraped the surface, but the shield had still dug hard into her arm with the weight of it.

Edita laughed and tossed back her loose dark hair. Her armour was black and luminescent, like the shell of a beetle, and it gleamed blue and green in the flickering light of the La Luminosa night lamps.

'Let's not postpone the inevitable, darling,' she sneered as Bianca clambered to her feet. 'With my idiot sister rotting in the catacombs with the other corpses, and little Catriona gone, you are all that stands in the way of my complete domination.'

Bianca blinked hard, refusing to shed the tears that threatened to blur her vision. She had already known her mother was dead. This changed nothing. Saralinda would want her to live.

'Now stand still and let me crush you!' Edita swung the mace again.

Bianca threw herself down and forward into a somersault that left her crouched at Edita's feet. *Thanks for the tip, Marco*, she thought. She stood up quickly, holding the shield over her head, and felt it connect with Edita's chin. The mace continued on its arc and Edita staggered back as it struck the floor of the piazza behind her.

'Brat!' Edita spat, and kicked out, catching Bianca on the shin with her hard, pointy, armoured boot. Bianca screamed as she felt her own skin tear and blood trickle down her ankle. 'You'll never be Duchess of Oscurita, *never*.'

Never wanted to be! Bianca thought, but she didn't have

the breath to shout it in Edita's face. Instead she made a desperate run for the street and the canal, dodging Edita's grasping hands. *She won't leave the battle to chase after me*, Bianca half thought, half prayed.

She was almost at the edge of the canal when she dared to glance back over her shoulder and saw that she was wrong. Edita was storming towards her, slapping aside La Luminosan soldiers who tried to stop her with powerful swings of her mace. Bianca panicked for a second, standing on the edge of the canal, unarmed and unprotected. Then she saw a winged shadow pass overhead. She didn't dare look up and draw Edita's attention to the skies . . .

'Catriona's alive!' she shouted. 'You said she was gone, not dead. That means she's still alive, and that means I can still save her!'

Edita stopped, alone on the street in front of Bianca. She lowered her mace, and laughed. 'She may not be dead yet, but you can't save her. I'll smash her, just like I've smashed all of your little toy soldiers,' she crowed.

The angel overhead dived, its golden sword raised to swipe at Edita's head. Edita swung the mace. Bianca gasped as it connected with the white marble. The angel shattered in mid-air and its pieces scattered across the street between Edita and Bianca, shards and dust raining down on them like snow. Edita moved towards Bianca, swinging the mace back and forth, a horrible grin on her face.

Bianca took half a step back and let out a tiny scream as she almost fell, but managed to steady herself. Her feet were right on the edge of the canal. The stones under her were slippery with hundreds of years of moss.

Edita advanced, and Bianca had no choice but to take a step forward.

'Say goodbye to your precious City of Light,' Edita said, and swung the mace. Bianca ducked under it and around until she was behind Edita. Holding up her shield, she shoved as hard as she possibly could.

The mace smashed into the stones of the canal bank and Edita went flying forwards. Losing her grip on the mace handle, she tripped and slid on the mossy stones, and fell into the canal with a huge *splosh*. She surfaced, gasping for air, and tried to claw her way back to land, but her black armour was weighing her down.

Bianca took hold of the mace's handle and just barely managed to work it out of the stones. While Edita was still splashing and struggling in the water, trying to release the buckles on the armour before she drowned, Bianca slowly and deliberately hefted the mace, staggered a few paces further along the canal bank, and threw it into the water. The mace sank.

Bianca watched Edita flail for a few more seconds, catching her breath and rubbing the place on her arm where the impact of the mace had hit her shield. She rather hoped that her aunt might do all the world a favour and sink under the canal surface, never to be seen again. But she was fighting – her helmet, breastplate, pauldrons and gauntlets had all come off and she was struggling with the neck-piece, which seemed to have tangled in her hair.

Bianca turned and looked back at the battle raging in the

piazza, thought for a second, and then blew a sharp whistle through two fingers. There was a scream, and then the huge black stone panthers broke from the battle lines and came trotting towards Bianca. She reached out to stroke their smooth heads.

'See that unarmed traitor? The one who's just sent all her armour to the bottom of the canal?' she said, pointing to Edita, who'd stopped struggling and was treading water, staring in horror at the big cats. 'Watch her closely, and don't let her get away. Think of her as a mouse. If she runs, you can chase her.'

One of the cats peeled its stone lips back to reveal a stone tongue and huge, sharp white marble fangs. The other one blinked at Bianca and a rumbling sound came from its enormous chest. Its purr was something like what Bianca imagined an avalanche would sound like high up in the mountains.

'Even without me,' Edita spat, 'my troops will crush your pathetic toy soldiers!'

Toy soldiers . . .

Bianca stared at Edita. 'Toy soldiers,' she repeated. 'You said you'd *smash* Catriona, like you smashed the angel . . .'

She backed away from the canal and stared at the poor angel's remains – the white marble chips, and the dust that looked a little like earth except that it was white, and when she picked it up between her thumb and forefinger it was made of tiny, sharp shards.

Just like the shards that had been in Duchess Catriona's room when she'd vanished. And just as there'd been in the horrible chamber in the Oscuritan catacombs, where the other half of the statues had all been smashed.

'That was your plan all along,' Bianca gasped. 'You sucked her into that statue somehow and you were going to smash it!' The shattered figures in the catacombs were all victims of the spell: real people transported into stone and destroyed by Edita. *But I won't let her smash Catriona!*

Bianca knelt down by the underwater craft, opened the hatch and scooped up the jar with the last of the special *animare* still swirling in the bottom like a living thing. She shut the hatch, glanced at Edita one more time, and then she broke into a run.

Chapter Nineteen

Bianca was sure she was right. She pictured the Oscuritan gift – Edita and Catriona's stone forms locked in an embrace. *Why? Why would Edita bother sending a gift?*

The question seemed to rattle around Bianca's mind: she should have asked it to herself as soon as the sculpture was unveiled. She sprinted through the empty streets of La Luminosa, making for the palace.

Why would Edita present Catriona with a statue as a token of Oscurita's friendship, when she knew the Baron would leave that very night and Oscurita would attack mere days later?

Because it was no ordinary gift.

She prayed with all her might to whatever saints and gods might be listening that she could fix it.

She was panting too hard to speak by the time she made it to the palace gate, but it creaked open as she staggered up to it.

'Huh,' she said to the two guards who stood by the gate. 'Thank you.'

One of the guards slipped off her helmet and gave Bianca

a solemn nod. 'We saw what you did with the statues, in the garden. Are you back to fetch more?'

Bianca nodded. 'Something like that.'

The other guard gripped his spear nervously. 'Lady Bianca, the battle . . . is it . . .?'

'Edita is down – but the battle's not over,' Bianca panted.

'Thank you,' said the female guard, and they both went back to watching the bridge.

Bianca hurried inside the palace and up the steps to the first floor and the Duchess's gardens. Her footfalls echoed as her feet slapped on the tiles in the empty corridors. She realised that the rooms were dark – even the night lamps hadn't been lit. A La Luminosan probably wouldn't have been able to make their way without lighting a torch, but Bianca could navigate by the bright, clear starlight that filtered in through the windows and the light from the glowing *animare* jar in her hand.

She stumbled out into the walled garden, her steps crunching on the gravel, and let out an audible sigh of relief. The statue was there, shining bright white in the starlight. Now that Bianca knew what she knew, Edita's embrace looked less like an expression of friendship and far more like she was reaching out to strangle Catriona.

Bianca started towards it, and then something moved and she skidded to a halt. On the bench in front of the statue, a figure was sitting, hunched. It turned around and looked at Bianca.

'Lady Bianca?' said Secretary Franco. 'Is that you?'

Bianca walked forwards, slowly. 'It's me,' she said. Bianca

circled around him, giving him a wide and wary berth, still heading for the statue of Catriona and Edita.

Then she saw the glitter of tears on his wrinkled cheeks.

'This is all my fault,' he said. 'I've failed Catriona, and I've failed La Luminosa.'

'Why would it be your fault?' Bianca asked.

'I didn't listen to you,' Secretary Franco said simply. 'I wanted to believe there could be peace. That Edita could be reasonable. All I wanted was peace, and now . . .' He trailed off, and in the silence Bianca could hear the clash and roar of the battle down in the city. 'Lord knows what has happened to the Duchess Catriona,' Franco went on. 'It was me who insisted on a diplomatic solution – and you knew better all along, didn't you?' He shook his head and ran his hands through his grey hair. 'I tried to unite the two cities once before, you know. I was idealistic. I thought a marriage between La Luminosa and Oscurita would solve all the problems of both cities. I persuaded the Duke to meet with your mother, Saralinda.'

'It wasn't your fault she fell in love with someone else,' Bianca said.

'But I knew the Duke didn't want to remarry. He let me talk him into it because he wanted peace as much as I did, but it was never a good idea. And then Edita made her first attempt to take the throne while Annunzio and Saralinda were here. So you see, all my fault from the very beginning.'

Bianca didn't say anything. It wasn't his fault – she thought it was rather obviously Edita's fault. But she could see he wasn't going to listen to reason right now.

'Oscurita fell into chaos, and when the Duke died, the Baron became Regent. I knew something was wrong when he had all of the Duke's most trusted advisors sent away. I played the fool, as if I hadn't known about Oscurita at all, and he believed me. When I realised what he'd planned to do to Catriona . . . I blamed myself, so I swore that this time I would help her to make peace with Oscurita, for good. I didn't learn my lesson. Now she's gone, maybe for good, and without her I don't know if La Luminosa can survive.'

Bianca held up the jar and unscrewed the lid. The *animare* tried to clamber up the sides and she nudged it back in with one finger.

'I have a crazy idea,' she said. 'Do you want to hear it?'

'Bianca,' Franco said, 'I'm ready to listen to you, as I should have done long ago.'

'I think Catriona's trapped in this sculpture. I think Edita's done this before. She was planning to get here before anyone realised what had happened, and smash the statue. I hope I can use this to wake Catriona and release her from this marble cell.'

Bianca waited for Franco to say something – perhaps 'what childish fantasy is this?' or 'be careful' or 'are you mad?'

'Then do it, for God's sake!' said Franco.

Bianca smiled. 'Do you still have the medallion?'

Franco fished in his pockets and pulled out the blank marble disc. He smiled at Bianca, and an expression she'd never seen him wear before crossed his face. It was . . . mischievous. 'Shall we take a leaf out of our dear Duchess's book?'

'Do it!' Bianca grinned.

Secretary Franco put the medallion down on the floor, seized his golden walking stick and brought it down hard in the centre of the disc. It splintered with a sound like wind rushing down a tunnel.

'Mmm?' said a muffled voice. 'Mm? Mm-*mmmmmm*!'

Bianca spun around. The voice was coming from the statue.

'I'm here, Catriona. Just hang on!' she said. She took a brushful of paint and carefully swiped it across Catriona's lips. She caught her breath – was she imagining it, or had there been a slight shimmer across the Duchess's skin? Was it just a cloud passing across the moon, or was the Duchess a slightly darker colour than the white marble on Edita's hands?

Bianca set to work, applying brushfuls of the magical paint to the Duchess, working it into her eyelids and across her cheeks. Catriona's colour was definitely coming back, her skin felt slightly soft to the touch. Bianca nudged the Duchess's dress with her knee and it shifted, like stiff fabric.

The transformation was slow, until suddenly it was done. Duchess Catriona blinked and let out a gasp and recoiled away from the grasping marble hands of Edita.

'What?' She staggered off the plinth and caught herself on a topiary bird. 'What the . . . What is going on?' She looked up at the dark sky, and then peered at Secretary Franco and Bianca. 'Why are we out in the garden? Why was I hugging that ugly thing?'

'You were under a spell, Your Highness,' said Secretary Franco.

'Oh! I remember!' Catriona gasped. 'I sat down on my bed, and I found this medallion, just like the one we smashed – and then it was like I fell *into* it. And then everything just went black.'

'Lady Bianca worked out Edita's plan and painted you back to life, Your Highness,' said Secretary Franco, with a kindly glance at Bianca.

'Oh, good,' said Catriona. 'Why's it so dark? And what's . . .?' She turned, following the sound of battle.

'They have invaded,' said Bianca. 'Edita is down, but we're outnumbered, and the battle's still going.'

Catriona didn't say a word, but hitched up her skirts and strode from the garden. As her dress brushed past one of the hedges, the last shards of marble fell away and sparkled on the leaves.

Bianca and Franco ran after her.

'Bring me a horse,' Catriona shouted as she entered the courtyard. 'And my armour!'

'Your Highness!' The two guards on the gate almost dropped their spears in surprise. 'Where did you . . .? How did . . .? I mean . . .' The guard remembered herself under Catriona's intense glare. 'Yes, of course, right away, Your Highness!' She ran off, leaving Catriona tapping her foot impatiently, and appeared a few minutes later leading a white horse laden with Duchess Catriona's golden armour. The guards began to help buckle Catriona into it, but Catriona held up a hand.

'Split it between me and Bianca,' she said. She glanced at Bianca. 'That is, if you're coming?'

'Try and stop me.' Bianca grinned and accepted the guard's help to put on the armour's shoulder plates while Franco helped Catriona fasten the breast plate. Then Duchess Catriona swung herself up onto the horse, helped Bianca up behind her, and drew her sword from the sheath.

'Not going to tell me to hang back and stay safe, Secretary Franco?' she asked, looking down at him with a twitch of her eyebrows.

'I wouldn't dare, Your Highness,' said Secretary Franco with a low bow.

Duchess Catriona laughed, and kicked the horse into a gallop. Bianca had to cling on to the Duchess's waist to stop herself from sliding off as they barrelled across the bridge and along the cobbled streets towards the sound of battle.

As they approached the piazza, they saw two large, black shapes in the street by the edge of the canal. The horse slowed and bucked as they looked up and blinked their large yellow eyes at it. Catriona gave the horse a soothing pat and then drew level with the panthers. For a second, Bianca panicked, unable to see Edita. Then she did: her treacherous aunt was lying on her back, her hair splayed across the cobbles, still breathing, but with one great stone paw resting casually – but heavily – across her chest.

Catriona paused to make sure Edita had seen her, then kicked the horse into a canter.

'Ready?' she said to Bianca.

'Ready . . . -ish,' said Bianca, as the horse's muscles bunched underneath her and it sprang forward.

For a moment, nobody seemed to notice the arrival of the Duchess. From on top of the horse, Bianca could see the battlefield, and her heart soared as she realised that the numbers were fairly even. A little pocket of Oscuritan soldiers were defending a corner of the piazza, with the Baron da Russo on his big black horse right at the back screaming orders at them to attack. But another group of Oscuritans were running away, retreating back into the museum. She thought she saw golden La Luminosan armour inside – they'd be taken prisoner, or perhaps forced back through the doors in the paintings. Bianca scanned the battle for Marco, and didn't see him, but she did catch one of the stone lions taking down a whole group of Oscuritan soldiers.

A soldier in silver ran towards Duchess Catriona, his sword raised, but Bianca kicked out and caught him on the side of the head with her newly armoured foot.

'God bless the Duchess!' Bianca yelled. 'Duchess Catriona is with us!'

Every head in the square turned. Every La Luminosan who could still raise their voice broke into a cheer. Bianca saw Captain Raphaeli, his helmet knocked off and his horse gone, blood-spattered but still fighting, raise his sword and take up the cheer before twisting to parry a thrust from an Oscuritan soldier. And finally, brilliantly, Bianca saw Marco. He was wielding an oar as if he'd trained with a staff all his life, and the tiny stone dragons were swarming around him, clawing and scratching at any Oscuritan who came close.

'God bless the Duchess!' Bianca heard him yell, as he spun the oar around his head and swung it down to knock the helmet clean off one of the enemy soldiers.

'God save La Luminosa!' cried Duchess Catriona. She kicked the horse forward, drew her sword, and charged.

Chapter Twenty

The red light of the sunrise seemed to dribble down between the buildings into the Museum Piazza, as if it wasn't in any hurry to illuminate the scene that lay below.

Bianca sat on the edge of the fountain, holding on tight to Marco's hand.

The fallen silver and golden soldiers mingled, lying side by side or sprawled on top of each other. The pinkish light and the spatters of blood made them all look the same colour. Wrinkled faces lay beside youthful ones, flesh and marble dust mixed together.

Bianca didn't want to look, but she couldn't shut her eyes to the horror of it.

'We won,' said Marco, quietly.

Bianca simply nodded. She couldn't make herself speak. With so many dead, it didn't look how she thought winning would look. And it certainly didn't feel good.

If I'd really known what war was, she thought, *I might have had more sympathy for Secretary Franco. Peace at any cost is not real peace . . . but he was brave for trying to make it work.*

Those who were able, picked through the bodies, searching for anyone they could still help, while priests and soldiers worked together to sort out the dead.

Bianca saw Cosimo and Lucia hobbling towards the stall that had been set up to tend to the walking wounded, supporting each other. Cosimo was bleeding from a shoulder wound, and Lucia was limping on one foot. Rosa and Ezio followed them, looking worn and sad but not physically injured.

'Dad's going to marry Olivia,' Marco said, almost casually. 'He proposed the instant the victory was called. Typical actor.'

Bianca tried hard to smile, but she wasn't sure it actually reached the outside of her face.

'Also,' said Marco, squeezing her hand, 'you were brilliant, and so was I, and we won, because of you. And me. Also, the Baron's dead, so there is that.'

Bianca nodded. 'Yeah,' she said quietly. 'There is that. Edita's in prison. The Oscuritan soldiers who lived are under arrest.' *We are out of danger, and that is enough*.

'Look, here comes Raphaeli,' Marco said.

Bianca looked up as the Captain walked over. His noble face bore a few bloodstains, but she didn't think any of it was his. This time, she managed to smile properly. She didn't need to tell him that he was her father right now. She'd let things settle a bit before she broke the news. For now, all she needed was the fact that he was alive and unharmed.

'Bianca,' said Captain Raphaeli. 'I . . . I'm so . . . that is –'

Bianca blinked at him, slightly stunned by this tall, powerful, blood-spattered Captain of the Guard seeming to be lost for words.

'You magicked up reinforcements when we were desperate for them. You fought off Edita by yourself. You brought Duchess Catriona back to us. I'm just . . . so, so impressed.'

'Thank you,' Bianca said quietly.

'May I have a word?' the Captain said. 'Alone?'

Marco raised an eyebrow at Bianca. 'I'll go and help . . . someone,' he said, and slipped away.

Captain Raphaeli took Marco's place on the fountain beside Bianca.

'I'm afraid I've been an unforgivable idiot,' he said. 'I had all the pieces, and I just didn't . . . allow myself to put it together until I saw you with Edita on the battlefield. The family resemblance is undeniable. You look like your aunt and your mother, so much so I can't believe I didn't see it before. But you said that your mother was the true Duchess, and my Sara was just a painter's apprentice.' The Captain gave a sad smile. 'Or that's what she told me . . .'

Bianca took a deep breath. 'Sara was Saralinda,' she said. 'The true Duchess. She came to La Luminosa in disguise.'

Captain Raphaeli ran his hands through his curly hair. 'I still can't believe it,' he said. He looked at Bianca. 'I'm your father. I have a daughter. And my daughter . . . is *incredible*.'

Bianca's eyes swam with tears. She wasn't sure if she was happy, or sad, or both, or simply more exhausted than she'd ever been in her life. But she had a father. A *great* one.

She shifted closer to him and he put his arms around her. She rested her head on his plate armour and felt like she'd finally come home.

'Listen,' her father said, without letting her go, 'I . . .

202

I understand that a Duchess can't just take up with a commoner. Especially one she's not seen for twelve years. Perhaps she has a Duke, now – I don't know. And I don't expect anything from her. But do you think she would be willing to see me? I loved her so, so much. If I could just see her again . . .'

The sob that Bianca had been holding on to while he spoke broke out of her, and she wept bitterly. Her father pulled away from her and looked into her face, his own face falling.

'Bianca?'

Suddenly there was a commotion across the courtyard. Someone shouted, 'They're coming through!' and there was a confused clatter from inside the museum. Captain Raphaeli held Bianca's face firmly for a long second and then jumped to his feet, his hand on his sword hilt.

'What's happening?' he demanded. 'Who's coming through?'

'Make way!' called an oddly familiar voice. Bianca stood and staggered over to look into the museum, and saw a man and a woman in dark grey cloaks step out of one of the paintings. Behind them, another cloaked woman helped a figure in black down from the doorway.

'We come in friendship – *true* friendship,' said Pietro, throwing back his hood. He was wearing thick glasses with dark coloured lenses. 'With the true Duchess of Oscurita.'

'Mother!' Bianca ran through the museum doors and skidded to a halt, just short of crashing into her. Saralinda was leaning heavily on the arm of the Resistance fighter who'd helped her down, and blinking against the glare of the morning sunshine. She had her right arm bandaged tightly to her shoulder, and she looked as if a stiff breeze could blow her over.

But she was alive. Saralinda was alive!

'Stand down!' Bianca yelled back at the La Luminosan soldiers who'd gathered around the museum entrance. 'This is the rightful Duchess of Oscurita, she's not your enemy.'

'Bianca,' Saralinda croaked, and reached out her arms.

'You're alive!' Bianca sobbed, stepping into the hug and embracing her mother as gently as she possibly could. 'Edita said you were dead!'

'My friends saved me.' Saralinda smiled. 'And we realised that the traitor Filpepi had given us a precious gift. Edita believed me dead, and without me the Resistance could be no threat, so she left almost nobody behind to guard the castle. She had no idea how many of her guards and her servants were truly supporters of mine – or willing to swear it, once I sat on the throne again. And you did the rest.' Saralinda gave a weak but bright grin. 'My brilliant girl.'

'Mother,' Bianca said, 'there's something else. I . . .'

She found she didn't know how to say it, so she just looked up at Captain Raphaeli. Saralinda followed her gaze. Her hand clutched hard onto Bianca's shoulder, and Bianca realised she might be about to faint. She met the Resistance fighter's eyes, who lowered Saralinda gently to the ground.

Raphaeli stepped forward. 'Sara,' he said, and fell to his knees in front of her, tears streaming down his face, leaving clean tracks through the grime of battle.

'Alessandro!' Saralinda gasped. 'My own Alessandro!' She reached for him, and he gently took her in his arms and kissed her.

Bianca stood, flushing with happiness and a twinge of embarrassment.

'Make way for the Duchess!' cried Secretary Franco's voice from the piazza, and Bianca almost skipped to the doors of the museum. Duchess Catriona was striding towards them, still half dressed in her golden armour, with Franco scurrying after her and Marco strolling in their wake.

'I hear we have a visitor?' She grinned at Bianca and linked their arms as she passed, dragging Bianca along. Bianca was glad to see that her parents had stopped kissing, and her mother was on her feet again, leaning on her father and beaming. 'Your Highness,' said Duchess Catriona, and for perhaps the first time in her life she dropped into a low, sincere curtsey.

'Your Highness,' echoed Saralinda, bobbing a weak curtsey back.

Duchess Catriona stepped forwards and placed her hands over Saralinda's. 'I am so pleased to meet you – the rightful Duchess of Oscurita, restored to her throne! I hear that you and my dear, late father were good friends,' Catriona said, beaming. Bianca glanced at Secretary Franco, and he nodded. He'd told her the truth then – her father hadn't wanted to remarry and instead had given his blessing to Saralinda's marriage for love.

'He was the best of men,' Saralinda said. 'And he loved you very much.'

'Ugh,' Catriona sniffed. 'Don't, I shall cry! I haven't cried yet today and I don't plan to start now. The question is, how shall we celebrate your re-coronation, Your Highness?'

'Actually,' Saralinda said, squeezing Captain Raphaeli's arm, 'as pleased as I am that my struggle is over and my usurping sister is off the throne . . . I honestly have no taste for leadership any more. It's been a long, long twelve years. Oscurita is ready for new blood. Young blood. It's time.'

They all turned to look at Bianca.

'Hey, hang on.' Bianca held up her hands. 'I'm not really duchess material! I totally failed as a lady.'

'Oh rubbish,' said Catriona, fixing her with her very best mischief-making smile. 'You've saved both our cities several times over in the last few days, I think you can handle sitting on a chair and making boring decisions about cleaning up canals.' Then she leaned close and murmured in Bianca's ear. 'Anyway, being a duchess is *much* better than being a lady.' Bianca actually *felt* her grin again. 'The Duchess is the one in charge . . .'

Epilogue

Bianca cackled with laughter as she turned the corner and saw the door to di Lombardi's secret workshop in front of her.

'Yes! I win, I win, I absolutely *crushed* you both,' she said, leaning on the wall and waiting for Catriona and Marco to catch up with her. They were only a few steps behind.

'I think being related to di Lombardi might be cheating,' Catriona said, narrowing her eyes at Bianca. 'I think this place just *likes* you better!'

'Isn't it the first *inside* the workshop who's the winner?' Marco gasped.

The three of them looked at each other, and then fell into a mad scramble of elbows and feet, trying to be the first through the door. Bianca fell through first and Marco landed on top of her.

'I still win,' she groaned.

Duchess Catriona stepped daintily over both of them, and then collapsed onto a stool with a giggle. 'I suppose I can live with that,' she said. 'As long as you don't make a habit of it. And as long as the *filthy traitor* doesn't win,' she added, glaring at Marco.

'That's a bit strong,' Marco complained. 'Just because you're jealous. Bianca invited me, you know!'

'Well, it doesn't make any sense,' Catriona said, throwing her hands in the air. 'How *can* you be taking your new show to Oscurita first? Your troupe won't even be able to see what they're doing!'

'Torches,' said Marco simply. 'Lots and *lots* of torches.'

'It's going to be *amazing*,' Bianca teased. 'They're going to do everything twice, and backwards, and on *fire*.'

'Why, Duchess Bianca, I think the power's gone to your head,' said Catriona.

Bianca laughed. 'Anyway,' she said. 'You know how important it is. Art in Oscurita has been suppressed for years and years. I've got to get people interested in music and performance and magic and painting again. What better way than to show them what Master Xavier's Harlequin Troupe can do?'

'It doesn't seem very fair to me, Bianca,' said Catriona. 'You've already stolen away the most promising young artist of her generation and shoved a crown on her head. You can't have Marco as well. Marco's mine. So there.'

'As much as I enjoy listening to you two argue over me,' Marco grinned, 'it's your day off! Do you really want to waste it bickering . . . or do you want to come and see what I found in the back of the workshop?'

'Another contraption?' Bianca beamed as he led them towards something about as tall as a horse and twice as wide. It was hidden underneath a white dustsheet. When he was sure they were watching, Marco drew the sheet aside with a flourish.

It was something like a chariot, Bianca thought. The cart section gleamed golden and purple, with a wide bench seat upholstered in comfortable-looking velvet. And at the front, where the horses should have gone, there was a glass orb, a bit like a fishbowl, full of strange pipes and gears and springs and bellows.

'It powers itself!' Marco grinned. 'You just get into it and *go*!'

Bianca and Catriona exchanged sceptical looks.

Marco wiggled his eyebrows at them.

'Do you want to take it for a ride?'

Imogen Rossi

Imogen Rossi grew up in London but her favourite place in the world is Venice during the Carnival. She spent most of her summer holidays in Italy, where she passed the time doodling and writing stories. She loves to paint, though she isn't very good at it, and she sings in a choir. She most enjoys stories involving mystery, magic and time travel. She has a collection of Venetian carnival masks and two cats named Leonardo and Michelangelo (Lenny and Mike for short).

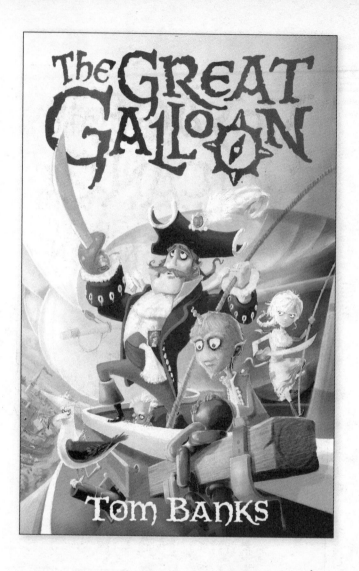

THE GREAT GALLOON

TOM BANKS

The Great Galloon is an enormous airship, built by
Captain Meredith Anstruther and manned by his
crew, who might seem like a bit of a motley bunch
but who are able to fight off invading marauders
whilst drinking tea and sweeping floors!

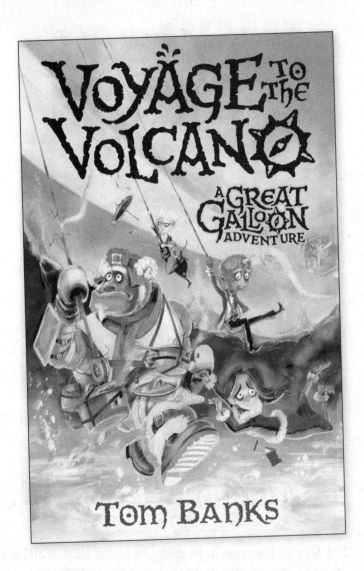

**Captain Anstruther and his motley crew of
sky-pirates are back for more adventures!**

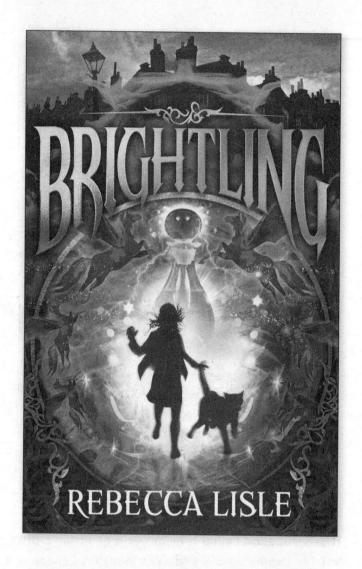

A fantastical reimagining of OLIVER TWIST,
featuring a feisty orphan called Sparrow,
very good goodies and very bad baddies, and a
mysterious glowing substance called Brightling ...

Jill Paton Walsh

FIREWEED

Foreword by Lucy Mangan

It's 1940, and London is in the grip of Hitler's Blitz, but for runaways Bill and Julie wartime London is a playground. Although ducking Nazi missiles and camping in bombed-out houses seems almost fun for a while, the reality of living through a war quickly begins to set in. Winter is coming, and Bill and Julie will discover that playing at being grown-ups can be a very dangerous game indeed ...

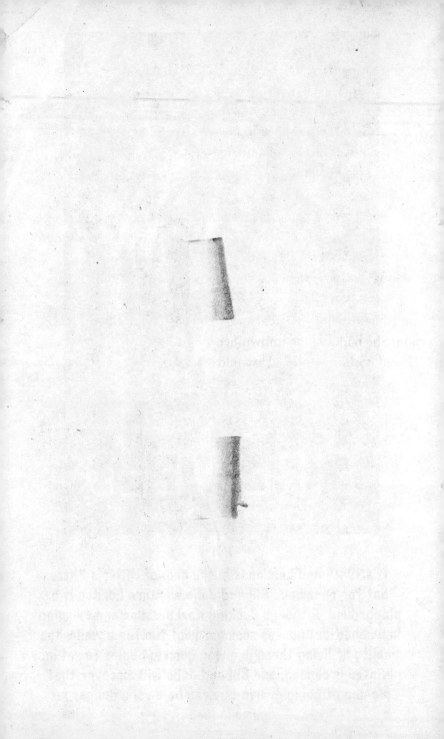